INTO
THE
WILD
NERD
YONDER

INTO THE WILD NERD YONDER

BY JULIE HALPERN

SQUARE
FISH

FEIWEL AND FRIENDS
New York, NY

SQUARE FISH

An Imprint of Macmillan

Library of Congress Cataloging-in-Publication Data
Halpern, Julie,
Into the wild nerd yonder / by Julie Halpern.
p. cm.
Summary: When high school sophomore Jessie's long-term best friend
transforms herself into a punk and goes after Jessie's would-be boyfriend,
Jessie decides to visit "the wild nerd yonder" and seek true friends
among classmates who play Dungeons and Dragons.
ISBN 978-0-312-65307-1
[1. Best friends—Fiction.   2. Friendship—Fiction.   3. Popularity—
Fiction.   4. High schools—Fiction.   5. Schools—Fiction.
6. Brothers and sisters—Fiction.   7. Dungeons and dragons (Game)—
Fiction.]   I. Title.   PZ7.H1666Rol 2009 [Fic]—dc22   2008034751

Originally published in the United States by Feiwel and Friends
First Square Fish Edition: April 2011
Square Fish logo designed by Filomena Tuosto
Book designed by Lorie Pagnozzi
macteenbooks.com

P1

AR: 5.4

To my Dungeons and Dragons kids,

past, present, future, and every plane in between

I wanna see movies of my dreams.

—*Built to Spill*

chapter 1

I SO USED TO LOVE THE FIRST DAY of school. Ever since my mom let me pick out my first pair of first-day-of-school navy Mary Janes with the flower pattern puckered into the top, I knew I'd like the newness, yet revel in the sameness that the first day of school always brings. New pens I'll lose after first period, new schedules with the promise of a cool new teacher or intriguing new exchange student, and new classes to ace. Not in a braggy, nerdy way, just in an I'm-smart-and-I-kind-of-like-to-study way. It's not as though school defines me. Although, I guess I don't really know *what* defines me. Yet. Not like my best friends, Bizza and Char. Would it be lame to say that they define me?

Elizabeth Ann Brickman, or Bizza as she's been called since birth. (So I ask you: Why not just name her Bizza? I guess for the same reason my parents named me Jessica but call me Jessie. It's not really the same thing, though. Jessie's a pretty common name for an equally common girl. Unlike Bizza, uncommon in every way. Maybe that's why her mom decided to dub her only child Bizza, like how famous people name their kids after fruits and various other random unnamelike nouns—guaranteed un-anonymity.) Is it a name that lets someone know they're going to be different? Is it her name that makes her cocky and clever, weird but cool, funny but scary at the same time? Can a name do all of that? Or is it that everyone at Greenville High School knows Bizza because Bizza makes herself be known? If I truly wanted to, could I become infamous, too?

Not that I want to, but could I?

And then there's my other best friend, Char, who doesn't seem to have to try at all. Full name: Charlotte Antonia Phillips, every bit as gorgeous as her name implies, thin, but not skinny, tall, but not imposing, and hair so thick you could use it for climbing when in distress. If she were popular in the traditional high school use of the word she would be head cheerleader or prom queen or, I don't know, whatever else it is those "popular" people aspire to become. (Why are they referred to as "popular" anyway? That would suggest that everyone likes them, which is virtually impossible since popular people are notorious for treating the commoners like crap.) But popularity among the masses has never been anything that Bizza, Char, or I have aspired to. Which is why we've always been such great friends.

It started in first grade when the three of us convinced our teacher that the other students' lives would be empty without our fabulous lip-synching rendition of the movie *Grease,* so we gathered up any first graders willing to dance in front of people (amazing how it was so easy back then to find boys who weren't ashamed to dance) and any girl who was fine being relegated to one of the random, nameless Pink Ladies in the background. Bizza mouthed Rizzo's parts, Char mouthed Sandy's, and I was usually the Twinkie-loving Pink Lady Jan. At least my Pink Lady had a name, right?

Bizza, Char, and I have always had this fantastic creative energy, and a lot of funky things were born out of our friendship. In seventh grade we filmed one episode of a soap opera we created called *Mucho Love* (based on the *telenovellas* our Spanish teacher, Señora Goldberg, showed us in class). The soap was so funny, we actually got it aired on cable access (although I think cable access channels are legally required to air anything anyone sends them). Of course, *Mucho Love* wouldn't have been nearly as good if Bizza and Char hadn't convinced all of the hotties on the block to play the studly male leads. But that's why we work(ed) so well together: I bring the brains, they bring the brawn.

In eighth grade we started a band, The Chakras (Char thought it sounded "mystical"), and we all took up instruments. Bizza was, of course, the lead singer (without a care in the world that her voice sounded like the cries of a llama taking a particularly painful dump) and guitarist (her guitar playing wasn't much better than her singing). Char was the statuesque (and statuelike, since the only things she moved were her fingers) bass player. ("Chicks are always bass players," was her reasoning. My response: "Um, aren't we all chicks?") And I was the drummer, pounding away in the background. I didn't actually mind, since I was playing on Van Davis's drum kit. (Sigh.) And I'm pretty good. I think it goes along with my crazy math abilities. Sadly, The Chakas broke up after Bizza and Char decided that it was more interesting telling people we were in a band than actually practicing. They *still* tell people we're in a band. "But we're on hiatus." Bizza's words.

Now that we're in high school, being friends with Bizza and Char means I get invited to parties by the likes of Gina Betancourt and can experience firsthand what it's like to watch drunk people puke. It also means that at any of said parties, I practically don't even have to get dressed or fix my hair (not that it would matter anyway, since there is nothing I can do to perkify its straight brown blahness) because no one notices me anyway in Bizza's or Char's presence. Which I consider a good thing, most of the time.

But things are starting to change.

Last year, freshman year, I had the genius plan to start a sewing business. My mom has always made funny clothes for me, mainly for Halloween, but sometimes for other festive occasions (I look back fondly on my Arbor Day beret), and she taught me to sew last summer. My idea was to create simple, A-line skirts using a basic sewing pattern, but making them out of all of the hilarious fabrics they sell at fabric stores. It's insane what the bizarro fabric creators come up with (whose job is that anyway?): Jelly bean fabric. Prairie dog fabric. Coffee lover's fabric. They even have fabric for hunters: deer awaiting tragic death as they hang out in the woods. What kind of hunter would wear that pattern? Maybe hunters' wives like to make their hunter husbands little hunter pajamas. How quaint.

I thought the skirt thing was an obvious great idea, and Bizza and Char humored me for all of two days. Then they decided it was just "too home ec," and they'd rather hang out at the local Denny's. Denny's is where my brother, Barrett (two years older, completely adorable, the only boy at school with an orange mohawk), and his freakster friends hang out, drink coffee, and smoke (not Barrett, though, who believes, and I quote, "I'd rather my mouth tasted like the zebra-y goodness of Fruit Stripe gum than of someone's ass"). Barrett took me to Denny's a few times last year, trying to be all big brotherly, but it wasn't really my scene. His friends, for the most part, are pretty nice to me. Instead of looking through me (like the people at Gina Betancourt's party), they usually try to include me in their conversations. But their conversations are about music ninety-nine percent of the time, and I don't care enough about the Scrapheaps or the Turdmunchers or the Firepoos (I may have some of the names incorrect, due to my entire lack of interest) to converse about them. Ironically, I have filled in for the drummer (the aforementioned and insanely gorgeous Van) of Barrett's band, the Crudhoppers, during several practices, but I don't really listen to the music we're playing. That may sound impossible, but I'm so busy counting and trying to keep up the punk-fast pace that I don't really have the option of listening. It's funny how some of Barrett's friends think I'm his punky kid sister, when really I'm just some mathlete who'd rather be sewing Thanksgiving skirts in her bedroom while listening to an audiobook.

I glaze over the Crudhoppers' Denny's conversations and try to hold in my coughs as Van and Pete Mosely puff smoke rings and stank up my clothes. Bizza and Char, however, think the Denny's smoking section is the absolute of cool and berate me every time I fail to invite them when Barrett drags me along. (I also fail to mention to them that after Barrett invites me, he says, "Jessie, why don't you leave the two poseurettes at home tonight." Part of me feels guilty because I know they want to be there, but part of me thinks I deserve to be the attention girl, even if it is covered in a cloud of smoke.)

The worlds of the poseurettes and the freaksters collided this summer when Bizza decided that a nightly hang at Denny's was a must. Gaggingly, she even picked up the classy habit of smoking because "it's the only way we'll look cool sitting in the smoking section." Char bought a pack of clove cigarettes, claiming they tasted good, to which I ask why doesn't she just go suck on a clove so I don't have to inhale her perfumed secondhand smoke? Not to mention the damage it can do to my skirts. Even though Bizza and Char would rather make holes in their lungs (and mine) than make skirts, I am still way into the sewing. My goal is to sew enough skirts this summer to have a different skirt for every day of the school year. So far I have over seventy skirts (including skirts I started last summer, but not including the fifteen or so I made and sold at our school's summer craft fair). Bizza and Char have been too busy trying to infiltrate Barrett's crew to notice.

The final month of summer became a smoky Denny's extravaganza. The 'Hoppers were there almost every night, and since Bizza had made her mind up, *we* were there every night, too. Such a bummer because the end of summer is usually so amazing. Yeah, the back-to-school sales are unbelievable, but there's also something about the August air that's the perfect blend of summer and fall. It's so warm and wonderful. Bizza, Char, and I have spent every August since forever together in Bizza's backyard "tree house" (a floor of wood shoved into the top of her weeping willow tree) looking up at the sky and playing Would You Rather? Now I play Would You Rather? in my head every night we're at Denny's:

Would I rather
a) Be in the Denny's smoking section
b) Eat a live turtle, shell included
c) Lick a turkey's ass

Yeah. Tough call these days.

I have always held a mix of admiration and embarrassment for Bizza. It's amazing how she gets people to pay attention to her, something I could never do, and how she thinks she is so good at everything. Even when she sucks (as in her singer/guitarist days), she thinks she's a star. When she gets a seventy-five on a test, she thinks it's because the teacher doesn't know how to teach. And when a guy doesn't like her (god forbid), he's *obviously* gay. And on one dark and smoky night when Barrett drove the three of us to Denny's, she somehow managed to convince him that it would be acceptable to let us join the Crudhoppers' table. When we arrived at the smoky booth, Bizza gestured to me with her eyes as though I was supposed to introduce, or maybe even *announce*, her.

"Um, hey, guys." I tried to sound casual.

"Hey, Jessie." Van smiled. I always wondered if the reason Van was nice to me was because Barrett told him that I'd had a major crush on him since sixth grade. I had been borderline crushing on him for a while, as younger sisters do on their brother's friends, but then I had this über-romantic dream about him, which changed the status from borderline to obsessed. Van has this amazing smile, a freaky cool crooked nose, and dark hair that looks so perfectly imperfect. "Who are your friends?" Van asked, smacking me back into the reality that almost anyone is more interesting than me.

"This is Bizza. This is Char." The guys smiled and nodded as the girls charmed their way into the squished booth. I pulled up a chair. Coffees were ordered (loaded with cream and sugar), cancer sticks were puffed, and conversation followed the usual, musical route, but with many vapid Bizza interjections:

"That new Smokin' Chokes CD is shit. Why'd they replace Emery Gladen?" A 'Hopper mused.

"I love the new color of your hair, Van. How do you get it to stay so black?" Bizza blathered. This could have bothered me more, except any conversation between Bizza and a guy sounds flirty. Kind of annoying, but meaningless and completely the norm.

"We gotta get ready for our show at the Interoom. Our new songs aren't tight enough," a 'Hopper suggested.

"Did you get those shoes at Nordstrom, Eric? I totally saw them there. I almost got the same ones," Bizza noted importantly.

Each summer night was filled with identically inane conversations. All I wanted to do was stay home and sew, and look forward to the joyous day that I'd go back to school and homework and all of the smart-girl excuses I get to use so as not to waste my life at Denny's every night. I frequently tried telling Bizza that I had some sewing I wanted to finish this summer, but she would just say something like, "Whatever, Holly Hobby, you can sew later. We'll miss you if you're not with us," which made me feel simultaneously good and bad. Bizza is an expert at that.

So my final nights of summer were wasted with mediocrity and cigarettes. Barrett drove us to Denny's, Bizza acted like Bizza, and, as usual, her magical Bizzabilities charmed the pants off of them. Not literally, of course. The conversations turned away from music and moved to food, TV, movies—anything that Bizza deemed worthy of chatter. As the days went by, my skirts got smokier, and the weeping willow tree house got lonelier. Thank god, the summer is just about over.

Yeah, I used to like the first day of school. Until my best friends decided to turn punk.

chapter 2

WHAT THE BUTT? I ALREADY HAVE A Mr. Punk Rock Cool Guy brother; I don't need Punk Rock Wannabe friends. And today is their big debut: the first day of school, where summer can transform anyone and it's almost always accepted. Like Jenna Marny, who left school after eighth grade a fat, invisible nobody and came back a skinny, nose-jobbed somebody. Now she's going out with the captain of the soccer team. Or lacrosse. Or maybe both? Summer can do that to a person. Now Bizza and Char can be added to the list of the Great Transformed.

As I get ready for school (choosing a homemade skirt with pencils and rulers for first-day-of-school flare), I brush my straight brown hair, the same hair I've had for the past five years. (Obviously it's the same hair I've always had, but I mean the same "style." The only style, really, that my hair will do.) I sort of have a fear of trying anything different than shoulder length, parted a tad off to the side, ever since the Mushroom Cut Debacle of third grade. Who knew that, shortened, my hair would fluff up and become bizarrely fungi-shaped? The trauma left me with no choice but to leave my hair as is for the rest of my life, to ensure that nothing hair embarrassing ever happens again.

I experiment a little with some fun eye shadow colors and decide that green looks best with my brown eyes. I don't normally wear makeup because I'm too lazy and tired in the morning (and besides, what's the point? It's not like anyone else would notice.) but it's always easy for me to wake up on the first day of school. The excitement of new classes, seeing people who I like in an everyday way but not an outside-of-school way, and organizing my locker always springs me to life. Not to mention the joy of finally getting to legitimately use all of the school supplies that I've been hoarding for weeks. I follow every back-to-school sale in the Sunday paper, compare prices, highlight the ads, visit all of the necessary stores, and then hide the supplies in my genuinely worn, not faux-distressed, red backpack. I love opening the backpack on First Day of School Eve and—surprise!—there's all my new stuff.

I take one last look in the mirror before heading down to breakfast. I look kind of cute in my new skirt and eye shadow. Not much different than last year, but not all of us are dying to turn into someone else. Most of the time, anyway.

At breakfast, Mom and Dad run around, grabbing for newspapers and coffee cups. Both of them are teachers, although we like to refer to Mom as Doc, since she received her Ph.D. in education last year. I never quite understood how regular teachers could turn into doctors. (Like our old, horrid,

Southern gym teacher, Dr. Stunter. What did she have a Ph.D. in—Dodgeball? Rope climbing? Child torture?) until Mom spent three grueling years in night school. Not that I'm not grateful, since it forced Dad to hone his cooking skills and prove once and for all that a man's place is in the kitchen. At least in my house.

Dr. and Mr. Sloan always leave the house a little before me and Barrett, to uphold the appearance that all teachers do, in fact, live in their classrooms. Both of them are wearing suits, which they usually do for the first week or two of school to scare the children into thinking they're *serious teachers*. After that, it's all Dad can do not to wear his ratty old Cubs hat to work (to cover up his ever-expanding bald spot), although Mom usually at least wears skirts until the slush of winter forces her into cords. She keeps her makeup to a minimum, and her hair is straight and brown, like mine, but in permanent mom-bob. People always tell us we look alike.

Barrett slouches at the kitchen table, his Mohawk a faded, barfy orange, flopped over, sans gel. "You didn't fix your hair?" I ask him.

"I'm tired of it. Maybe I'll shave it off tomorrow."

"I like when you have hair, Barrett. Don't forget senior pictures. I don't want you looking like a skinhead," Doc Mom says. She kisses Barrett's head, then kisses mine, and says good-bye.

Dad grabs an apple and blows a kiss. "Happy first day!" he calls.

"Excited about going back?" Barrett asks. He knows how much I don't hate school.

"Yeah. Kind of," I say, not trying to sound too eager.

"Just kind of? What's the prob?" Barrett chomps on a Strawberry Frosted Pop-Tart (untoasted), his favorite.

"I'm just a little nervous about what it's going to be like this year."

"Same as last year for you. Now for me, the senior, this will be a year of college crap, followed by the joy of slackness once I get accepted to NYU."

All Barrett talks about is going to NYU next year; I don't even think he's applying anywhere else, although I don't want to ask him. Too momish. And the more we talk about him going away to college, the more I have to think about the fact that he'll be *going away to college.* "That's all well and good for you, Mr. Leaving His Sister All Alone, but I have to worry about the mortifying morphing of my friends."

Bizza's and Char's official physical transformations started this past week, when Bizza received a bunch of money from her mom for mowing the lawn all summer and doing other various around-the-house tasks that most other teens (i.e., me) don't get paid for. Bizza went straight to the Hot Topic in the mall and bought all of the kitschy T-shirts, skanky stockings, suspenders, studded jewelry, patches, buttons, and stickers mow money could buy. I wanted to tell her that, according to Barrett, any real punk would never set foot in a mall to buy their clothes. (Barrett gets everything he owns from thrift stores, punk shows, and online.) Char opted for a more vintage-looking mix of old dresses and a giant pair of combat boots she found in her attic (I think they might have been her dad's. They look really huge and make her walk a little like a tripping Frankenstein). She bought a ton of buttons of punk bands and covered her messenger bag. I guess this is how one dresses according to the overnight punk handbook.

"Ah, the poseurettes," Barrett smirks.

"Do you still think they're poseurettes? You *did* let them sit with the 'Hoppers at Denny's."

"I can't say no to your friends, Jess, at least not when they're already there. I knew them when they were Barbie toddling dorks. But I don't care how much Manic Panic they put in their hair, they'll always just be my little sister's friends."

I'm happy to hear he's not fooled by their punk-in-a-box makeover, but I wonder what everyone else will think.

I flip my Berry Berry Kix around in my bowl.

"Hey, don't look so worried. I'm sure they'll find something else to glom onto next month," Barrett tries to assure me. "And just think, if your friends are all punk, we'll be seeing a lot more of each other."

"Yeah, before you abandon me and go off to college."

"We have a whole year before I abandon you. Ready?"

"I guess." I grab my backpack, deflated without the weight

of homework, and head out in Barrett's car. Fugazi yells out of the stereo and onto the streets through our open windows. I watch myself in the side-view mirror, my straight hair poking me in the eye every minute or so. I hope it doesn't ruin my eye shadow. Why do I even bother?

chapter 3

THIS IS FAR WORSE THAN I EVER could have imagined. I'm at my locker, trying to remember the combination that I spun twenty times a day as a freshman, when a black figure lurks up on me. I see it out of the corner of my eye, but don't think much of it until I hear a creepy voice. "Jessie Sloan . . . Jessie Sloan . . ." It's like a ghost or a dream, but when I finally look, it's way scarier.

"Shit!" I jump. It's all I can say. Before me stands Char, her once-beautiful blond hair muddied with equal stripes of black and red. Her left arm is covered up to her elbows in black, ropey, studly bracelets. On her right wrist is—wait—a tattoo? Small black stars are etched neatly in a bracelet around her wrist.

"You got a tattoo?" I ask in an annoyed yet intrigued way. There are about a million more things I want to ask her, but I refrain. Do I even want to know?

"Yeah, well, sort of. It's a drawing. Van did it for me."

"Van?" Barrett's Van? *My* Van?

"Yeah. This weekend at Denny's. I said I wanted a tattoo, and he said he could give me one. Then he drew it. It's hot, right? He could have given you one, too, if you were there.

Touched your hand the whole time," she smirks. "Why didn't you come?"

I want to tell her that I was sick of listening to all of the nonconversations and inhaling the dirty air, but instead I just say, "I had to finish this skirt. You like?"

"Hmmm. It's cute. Funny," which I would have taken as a compliment, but she said it with such dismissal in her voice. I didn't say anything bad about her hair, so what gives? "Have you seen Bizza?" Char looks around.

"No. I don't know if she's here yet."

"Oh, she's here. I wondered if you've *seen* her. You'll die. She looks so cool."

I'll die, huh? Of what, exactly? My brain starts making a list of all of the twisted things Bizza could have done to garner even more attention. Then I catch her face coming my way down the hall. But what's missing? Ah yes, her hair. Bizza has shaved her head completely, so the only hair left is a soft layer of fuzz.

She holds herself so high that everyone in the halls can't help but notice. Her hair is gone. It's something I could never do, *would* never do. Without her hair, she looks like a different person. Just like Char does. And here I am: same as freshman year. And eighth grade. And seventh grade. Bizza looks so smug and confident and, dare I say, *punk*. And what am I again? Oh yeah, nothing.

"Hey, Jess, what do you think?" Bizza does a mock-fancy turn and runs her hand over the top of her buzz. She's truly interested in my answer.

18

I almost say that I actually think it looks kind of good, but I just can't. Usually I'm pretty generous with the compliments because why not try and make someone feel good? But there is something so annoying to me about this extreme hair show. "Fuzzy," I decide. She seems satisfied with the answer and quickly moves on to looking around the hallway for other reactions.

The first bell rings. "Better get to class, ladies. Mrs. Buxton always has a shitfit if I'm late. I can't wait to see her face when she sees this," Bizza muses, brushing the top of her hair with her palm.

The three of us head down the hall. People are packed together, hugging their beginning-of-the-school-year hellos. But as Bizza and Char walk, the crowd parts. I watch the innocent bystanders from behind Bizza and Char (walking with them would feel like a game of "Which one of these things doesn't belong?"). Some people point and laugh at them. Others' eyes bug out, and they turn away to whisper to their friends. One guy, I can't see who, yells out, "Freaks!" Bizza doesn't seem to care at all. I can almost see the defiant smirk through the back of her shaved head as she holds up her middle finger high and cuts through the hallway. I turn into honors English and wonder if Bizza remembered me in her moment of punk rock glory to turn around and share it with me. It's not like she shared her shaving experiment with me, so why would she include me in this? Why didn't she call me when she buzzed it? Did she think I'd try and talk her out of it? Make fun of her? Or maybe she just thinks my boring brown hair wouldn't understand.

The quiet normalcy in honors English is a welcome change from the new hair drama in my life. I sit down next to Polly Chlumsky, a familiar, friendly face from years of gifted classes together. Polly is a flute prodigy, which suits her perfectly. She sort of looks like a flute; everything about her is long and elegant—her hair, her nose, her fingers. I have only ever seen her play once, during an all-school assembly. It pissed me off how most of the students talked or slept during the performance because Polly deserved better. If it is possible to kick another flute player's ass, she definitely did just that. (By the way—I know a flute player is technically called a "flautist," but something about it sounds a little sketchy, as does "pianist," so I will refrain. If I need to refer to it in the future I will use the variant, "flutist," which also works. I looked it up.)

"Hey, Jessie, how was your summer?"

Well, Polly, my friends turned into poseur punk rock turdettes who didn't invite me into their personal hair club. Have you seen them? I'm sure they'll make an announcement about Bizza's haircut over the loudspeaker. And maybe they'll hold a pep rally. "Pretty good." I decide to just tell her the non-annoying parts. "I made about fifty skirts."

"Is that a new one? Very cute. Very 'first day of school.'"

Polly knows how to give good compliment. She always appreciated my occasion-appropriate fashion sense, and she actually bought one of my skirts at the Greenville High Summer Craft Fair. It had a bunch of fruit baskets all over it. I doubt she'll ever wear it, but it was nice of her to show her Gifted and Talented support. "I went to band camp for the first time." Polly laughs as she says this. "I know, I know. So cliché. And no, I did not stick my flute up you-know-where." I laugh. I think flutists worldwide will never live down the *American Pie* flute-in-the-crotch reference. "But I did meet a guy," Polly says. She opens up her neatly decorated binder, and taped to the inside is a picture of a guy with round glasses, a military haircut (short on top, even shorter on the sides—ugh), and a T-shirt that says "Science Olympiad 2008." Awkward. I hate when someone you like wants you to like something they like but you can't quite muster up the fakeness to tell them something, anything, good. This is one of those times. "His name is Jake," Polly gushes. "Isn't he cute?"

"Yeah." I smile, trying to look sincere. Polly leaves her binder open as Ms. Norton passes out this semester's reading list and class expectations. I look at the picture of Jake and try to see what Polly sees. Maybe he has a nice voice or he's really funny or crazy talented in whatever instrument he plays (I'm guessing the oboe). Did they kiss? Do more? I glance at Polly, and suddenly she looks about fifteen years older than she did two minutes ago. Summer sure can change people. Just not me.

chapter 4

I'M SLIGHTLY RELIEVED THAT I ENDED
up with fifth-period lunch, while Bizza and Char have seventh
period. I'd rather not have to deal. But that means that I either
have to walk around the cafeteria with a "pick me" look of
desperation while I try to figure out who I kind of know, or I
can sit outside on a bench and eat while I listen to an audiobook on my iPod. No-brainer.

I munch an apple as I listen to a particularly gory scene in
Stephen King's *Cell*, where a zombie-type person rips off another zombie-type person's ear. I'm pretty grossed out and
consider whether to *re*consider this as a listening choice when
I'm jerked away from the story by a grab on my shoulder. I
look up and see the gorgeousness of Van. He asks me something, but I can't hear him between the apple crunching and
the flesh biting. I yank out my earbud.

"Hi." I smile. "I didn't know you had fifth-period lunch,"
which, of course, makes it sound like I'm keeping track of his
schedule and I should have been more on top of things.

"Yup," he says, dangling his car keys from his finger.
"You want to get out of here?" I nod, trying not to look as in-

credulous as I feel. Going out for a second lunch with Van. My hands barely work as I grab my stuff and follow him to his car.

Greenville High School is located on a major road across from a million fast-food restaurants and car dealerships. If you want to go out for lunch, it's actually much faster to walk instead of having to deal with the onslaught of lunchtime traffic, but it's not nearly as cool. Van's car is what Barrett enviously refers to as "a classic pile of shit," a Gremlin, which for those who have never seen one is about the grossest, '70s-looking car on the planet. The outside of the car is a classic vomit green, while the inside is mustard yellow, yet it somehow looks cool. Probably because it belongs to Van.

Van is a somewhat legendary player (in the female sense, not in the actual instrument playing sense, so I guess I mean "playa," but writing that just looks like "beach" in Spanish) on the local punk scene, according to Barrett. Loyal to a fault with his guy friends (he once got into a fight with a group of skinheads when they called Barrett a fag), Van is somewhat looser when it comes to the traditional boyfriend/girlfriend thing. Practically every week Barrett would tell our family a dinnertime tale involving Van and (fill in girl-of-the-week's name here). I was never sure if Barrett did this because he thought the stories were actually amusing (they usually were) or if he was not so subtly trying to provide his little sister with a book full of Van precautionary tales. No matter how much crap Barrett talked about Van and le bimbo du jour, it didn't stop me from playing around a fantasy in my head that when I'm old enough (not like I'll catch up to him, but maybe he has a minimum age requirement for hookups), Van will declare his love for me, and tell me he's done with the hoochie-of-the-week program, and that he never wants to screw around with anyone else but me. *Très* romantic, I know. But it's hard not to turn to soup around a guy as annoyingly delicious as Van. He has that TV-show-bad-boy thing (he doesn't speak as much as he sighs and smokes) going for him, which I'm a total sucker for. All I can hope is that he has a thing for the plain, girl-next-door types (who the bad boys always seem to end up with on TV, right?).

All of this is going through my mind as I sit in Van's Gremlin, music too loud and smoke from Van's dangling cigarette clinging to my hair. We pull into the parking lot of Wendy's, and Van lets the car and stereo run until he finishes his cigarette. When he's done, he flicks it out the window and shuts off the car. I want to tell him that not only is smoking bad for him and everyone else around him but flicking the butt out the window isn't exactly good for the environment. I refrain. So instead, there's at least a minute of dead silence. "Hungry?" he smirks my way, and I turn to pudding, grateful I didn't declare a smoking ban.

"Sure," I answer, still full from my first lunch.

"It's my treat," he says, and I get the tiniest rumble in my stomach that this could be the date I've always dreamt about. I mean, he asked, he drove, and he's buying. The few guys I dated always asked and paid (but never drove because they were my age—usually had the humiliation ride from a parent), but those guys were not anywhere near Van status.

We get to the counter, and Van orders a four-piece-nugget Kids' Meal. "It's a good deal." He shrugs to the zitty adult behind the counter. "And the lady will have . . ."

The lady. Hee-hee. I say, "Just a Frosty. I'm not that hungry."

"A Frosty," Van repeats to the man, who gives him his total. Van pulls out his chain wallet and fingers the dollars inside. "Yeah," he draws the word out and looks at me, "do you think I could borrow a buck from you, Jessie? I'll pay you back." I'd give him a hundred dollars just for saying my name. "Wait—two bucks?" he asks as he realizes the extent of his shortage. I have now paid for more than my Frosty, but no biggie. People go dutch all the time.

We grab a table by a window. I sit down and spoon my Frosty while Van pumps out six tiny paper cups of ketchup. He sets them up on the table in a perfect line. "I love the stuff," he says. He pulls the toy out of his Kids' Meal, a bunny bobble-head from some forgettable kids' movie. He holds it up, jiggles it, and hands it across the table. "For you," he says. I am mesmerized by the giant bunny head. Van munches his ketchup-dipped fry, and I have to restrain myself from jumping across the table and kissing his full, slightly chapped, ketchup-dappled lips.

I hold the bunny, shake it, and smile. "Thanks. I'd put it

in my car, if I had one." I'm trying to be cool, when I really know that this bunny is going directly onto my nightstand so I can kiss it (i.e., *the spirit of Van*) every night before I go to sleep.

Van inhales his tiny meal, and in an instant the lunch is over. I don't even have time to finish my unwanted Frosty. "Better get back. Wouldn't want to be late for my first day of shop," Van chuckles.

"Yeah," is all I manage to say, not wanting to sound too dorkish by concurring with, "I wouldn't want to be late to precalculus."

The ride back is as smoky and loud as the ride there, and we get to the parking lot with two minutes to spare before class.

I look over at Van as he superinhales his cigarette. "Thanks for lunch," I say, "and my bunny." I waggle the bunny at him in a thank-you gesture.

"No problem," he breathes, blowing smoke out of the corner of his mouth. Then he leans toward me, and I ready myself for a dream kiss. His arm brushes my shirt and the tiniest corner of my chest (not that my chest has corners) as he pushes open my door. "Door sometimes sticks." He smiles, his face way too close to mine for not having any actual lip-connecting intentions.

"Oh." I blush. I get out and look at my watch. One minute before the bell. "See you around," I call over my shoulder as I run into school like a dweeb who hates to be late for class. I make it to my seat just as the bell rings.

Before Mr. Bowles begins class, I hear Mike Eastman a couple of seats over say, "Was somebody smoking?" I simultaneously hope that someone and no one thinks it's me.

chapter 5

WHILE BIZZA AND CHAR WOW THE
free world with their punk-rock selves during seventh-period
lunch, I have study hall. On occasion I have ditched study hall
to hang out in the lunchroom (when I know I won't get caught),
but I'm glad I have the excuse of first-day-of-school honors
classes homework to stay in. Not that they'd notice. I spied
Bizza in the hall before seventh (of course she didn't see me)
talking with a couple Crudhoppers, who seemed totally wrapped
up in her bald-is-beautiful look. I watched as she put a hand on
each guy's shoulder, completely sure that that's where her
hands should be. Of course, I totally froze when I could have
put my hand on Van's shoulder, or more. I mean, he did touch
a tiny portion of my boob, so that's gotta mean something,
right?

Study hall "teachers" (Are they really teaching us anything except how to fake bathroom passes?) at Greenville
High School are a crapshoot. Sometimes you get the motherly,
doting woman who just wants to give you bathroom passes
and is fine "as long as you talk quietly." Other times you get
the gym teacher who's so used to yelling all day that any in-

stance of a disturbance is cause for a shout and a detention. Today is the in between: a home ec teacher who doesn't take any BS excuse (too used to that with students trying to get out of her own classes), but not too concerned with the noise level.

I try to focus on my precalc, but my mind keeps floating back to my pseudo-date with Van. I must be drooling or something because I'm snapped back into reality when a girl's voice asks, "Where *are* you?"

I look next to me and notice for the first time that I am sitting next to Dottie Bell, one of the known weirdos of Greenville High. And junior high. And elementary. She isn't the weird that Bizza and Char want to be known for, but the kind who was just born odd. Her hair is strawberry blond, with the possibility of being quite pretty if it weren't for the clumping factor due to obvious unwashedness. She wears oddly colored corduroys no matter what the temp is, and never goes anywhere without her denim jacket, which is lovingly covered with a hand-drawn Lord of the Rings symbol (yes, I lose several cool points for knowing what it is). She's been in several of my classes, usually pretty friendly, but mostly in her own world. I've never really gotten to know her, probably because I never put in the effort. Or maybe because she always seemed a little strange and I worried that I'd get sucked into some conversation about things which I know nothing about (except *Lord of the Rings,* which I do know something about, but I'd rather not everyone else know I know).

"Where are you?" she repeats with a curious look.

"Nowhere, really," I reply hesitantly because I'm not quite sure if she wants to know what I'm thinking about or if she actually thinks I'm on some other, parallel plane. "Um . . ." I manage.

"Like, you're obviously thinking about something pretty sweet. Or some*one*?" She laughs in her lazy voice.

"How can you tell?" I would not put it past her to be a mind reader.

"You're twinkling, like on an old TV show." She wiggles her fingers in front of her eyes. "Twinkle, twinkle and shit." I laugh. "Do I know him?"

Hmmm. She asks like I'd know who she knows. Is there any reason for Dottie to know of Van? Although, really, how could anyone *not* know of Van?

"Maybe," I suggest. "He's a friend of my brother. We had lunch. And maybe a little more. I'm not exactly sure, to tell you the truth."

"Well, keep me posted." She instantly loses interest and begins writing in a tattered notebook. I curiously watch her write, nervous that my flakiness will become fodder for her blog (if she has one, which I'd bet a million dollars she does). Whatever she's writing, it's not in English. The letters are from our alphabet, but the words themselves are completely unfamiliar.

"What language is that?" I ask, and then recoil when I realize how nosy I'm being.

Dottie doesn't seem bothered. "I made it up," she says, still writing. "I call it Dottonian, after myself, of course. It's based on a certain alpha and numerical pattern. It's a secret language I use to write to my pen pals."

"Pen pals?" I haven't had a pen pal since we were forced to write to students in Mexico during seventh-grade Spanish class. The only things Lupita and I ever found to talk about were fruit and the color of our clothes. It did not make for very interesting (or long) letters.

"Yeah. I find them online through my blog." I *so* called it. "Only the chosen few get actual handwritten letters. Totally old school. I got the idea when I bought about ten sheets of *Star Wars* stamps and didn't know what I was going to do with them. After I framed a couple, of course. Anyway, I send out a letter in Dottonian, and whoever figures it out gets to be my pen pal."

"How many have figured it out?"

"Well, just the one so far. She's from Denmark. Way cool. Here—" Dottie pauses to fish around in her bag. She pulls out a stack of airmail envelopes held together with a rubber band. Flipping through them, she finds a picture. "Here she is."

The picture is of a gorgeous, Scandinavian-looking girl: tall, big shoulders, puffed pink lips. She's wearing a Renaissance Fair type costume, complete with corset and giant skirt. At least I think it's a costume. I've never been to Denmark.

"She's pretty," I tell Dottie. "Is she your girlfriend?" I don't know what compels me to ask this. I guess I just assume that if you're writing letters to some gorgeous Scandinavian, and she's sending you pictures, something must be up.

"No." Dottie laughs. "Although I bet Doug would get off on that." She shakes her head and puts the picture away.

"Who's Doug?" I ask.

"Doug Emberly. My boyfriend." She says this in a *duh* way, but I look at her with a shrug. "We've been dating for, like, two years. He was in our honors bio class last year." I nod with recognition, but I'm really thinking how I don't even remember *her* being in my bio class. A boyfriend, a beautiful foreign pen pal, her own language. Dottie Bell's not exactly what I predicted.

The bell rings, and I close up my untouched precalc homework. Dottie diligently stuffs and licks an airmail envelope. "See you later. *Fligirbig Snurip*." She blinks and walks off. Is she going to tell me what that means, or does she expect me to figure it out? Maybe it's a test, and if I can't solve it I'm an idiot. But if I can solve it, what does that make me?

chapter 6

MY EXPECTEDLY DISAPPOINTING
first day of school ends with Bizza subtly making her way to
my locker by yelling, "You wish, jockstrap!" to some faceless
letterman down the hall. "Can you believe that guy just asked
me out?" she yells to me and everyone else within the tristate
area. "Yeah, right."

"He asked you out?" I question, intrigued but skeptical.
"What did he say?"

"He said if I couldn't get a date for homecoming he'd trade
a BJ for a date."

Only Bizza could turn some jackass's disturbing sexual
suggestion into a guy asking her out. "Sounds like a catch," I
tell her as I sort my homework books into my backpack.

"What are you doing now?" she asks me. I used to love
hanging out with Bizza after school. We would always go to
her house (so we didn't get drowned out by the noise of the
Crudhoppers practicing. Plus, Bizza has better cable) and
watch *King of the Hill* reruns while drinking kiddie cocktails
(which were actually just Sprite and the juice from a jar of

maraschino cherries, always with a tiny paper umbrella. Actually, the same tiny paper umbrella each week, warped from cherry juice overexposure). Char could never make it because she had to watch her twin brothers after school, so Bizza and I had some tight, just-us times. Sometimes we'd write articles for our imaginary zine, *Von Rolio*, about what it would be like if we went to school with cartoon characters instead of real people. Sample *Von Rolio* articles:

- "Why I Want to Date Bart Simpson: an ode to bad boys, even if they are seriously underage"
- "Family Guy is fat and ugly. 'Nuff said."
- "Why Do All Anime Guys Look Like Girls?"

We have more titles than actual articles, which is why *Von Rolio* still holds the "imaginary" title.

We haven't worked on *Von Rolio* since the end of last school year and the beginning of my skirt assignment and Bizza's road to hair-gone-missing. As much as I'd like to get back into the zine, I can't help but assume that Bizza's undergrown hair has outgrown it.

"I already have a ton of homework," I lie as I stuff my backpack and lift it like it's a heavy set of weights for emphasis. I do have homework, but it's definitely manageable.

"On the first day? Sucks to be you. Why don't we just hang out for a little while? I could really go for a kiddie cocktail."

34

She smiles at me, and I'm sucked in by the Bizza charm, happy that some of the Bizza I know (and like) is still there.

"Okay. Sure," I say optimistically.

"But let's go to your house," she adds, already walking three steps ahead of me down the hall. "The cleaning people are at my house today. Mom hates when we get in their way." My house? We never have maraschino cherries at my house. But we always have the Crudhoppers.

Van appears right on cue as we're heading out of the school, Barrett beside him. "What are you two lovely ladies up to on this fine first day of school?" Van asks, and I simultaneously blush at him thinking I'm lovely and barf at him thinking Bizza is, too.

"Oh, ya know, just chillaxin," Bizza tells him.

"Cool, cool," Van responds.

Barrett shifts his weight impatiently. He's seen Van talk to girls before, but it's gotta be weird that it's somehow become his sister and her friend. "We're going back home to practice. You guys need a ride somewhere?"

"Totally. We're going to your house, after all." Bizza bats her eyelashes at Barrett, who smiles uncomfortably.

"We've both got cars. Who wants to ride with me?" Van asks me and Bizza like whoever goes with him wins the ride-with-a-sex-god contest. A contest that I'd like to win, of course, but can't think of how to say "me" without looking pathetic. Or pissing off Barrett.

Bizza doesn't miss a beat and says, "Ooh. I've never been in a Gremlin before. I'll go with you, Van." Without looking back at me, Bizza calls, "See you at your place, Jess." Somehow it didn't sound pathetic when Bizza said it.

Barrett looks at my stuffed backpack and generously takes it off my back. He weighs it against his own bag. "Damn, Jess, are they making you carve all your homework on stone tablets? What do you have in here?"

"Four textbooks filled with nine hundred pages each, for which we will only get through about two hundred pages this year."

"Trade you." Barrett switches his bag with mine. "So how was the big first day of sophomore year?"

"Average," I answer. "Most of the same people in my classes as last year, similar expectations. Shouldn't be too hard." I rewind through my day and remember, "I sat next to Dottie Bell in study hall. Do you know her?"

"I've heard of her. Isn't she the girl who tried to join the boys' gymnastics team because she refused to wear a leotard in public?"

I forgot about that. I don't blame her, really. Who wants to have to shave your pubes just to compete in a sport? Let alone the nightmare it would be when you have your period. "Yeah. That's her. Did you know she made up her own language?"

"Yeah? What's it called? Dorkese?"

"Clever. So that must mean you speak Asswipian," I retort.

"Sorry. I didn't mean to offend you and your new bud."

We reach Barrett's car and get in. He starts the engine with the radio at automatic blast, but I click it off.

"She's not my bud," I say defensively. "She just sits next to me in study hall. No biggie."

"I'll start to worry when you come home speaking in a frequency only dorks can hear."

"So you're saying you'd be able to hear it, then?" We go back and forth like that the whole ride home. It bothers me that Barrett keeps referring to Dottie, who he doesn't even know, as a dork. I think she may be interesting, in a somewhat freakish way.

When we get home, Barrett heads directly toward the basement. I take out my precalc book and spread out on the coffee table as I click on *King of the Hill*.

I do a couple of problems, no Bizza and Van. I get up for pop, no Bizza and Van. Precalculus finished plus an episode and a half later, Bizza and Van finally walk in together. Holding hands.

chapter 7

IF BIZZA HAD ANY HAIR, I'M PRETTY sure it would be messed up. She wears a cat-ate-the-canary grin, while Van looks as vacant and mysterious as ever. As soon as they see me, Van drops Bizza's hand and pushes his way to the basement. "S'later," is all he says, and I don't even know to whom.

"Did I miss anything?" Bizza plops herself down on the couch next to me. "Oh—I love this episode! When Peggy jumps from the airplane and her parachutes don't work! Hilarious!"

Only an evil slut would think someone breaking all of their bones is hilarious. I don't care if they're just a cartoon character. I don't want to let Bizza see that I'm jealous, though, so I try to be nonchalant as I ask, "What took you so long? Did his shitmobile break down?"

"No. We just took the long way home. I wanted to hear some of the Crudhoppers' demo CD, so he played it for me. While we parked in a parking lot . . ."

I brace myself.

". . . And made out! Aahhh! Isn't he so scrumptious!" She falls back against the pillows dramatically.

While I try to think of an answer to that question that does not include the words "no" or "shit," I calculate in my head the last actual time I professed my crush on Van aloud. The whole thing started back in seventh grade during a Bizza and Char sleepover. Bizza dared me to dance around the Crudhoppers' band practice in my new "Precious Littles" (I kid you not) brand bra and underwear set. I was almost through the basement door, Bizza and Char dying in a giggle fit at the top of the stairs, when I burst out crying. I confided to the two of them that I couldn't let Van see me in that dorky underwear if I ever wanted him to like me. That got a big "Oooohh!" from Bizza and Char, but like good friends they promised they wouldn't tell. Of course, I couldn't count on the same from my big brother, who heard the whole basement-stair melodrama. That month, Van was at our house for dinner, and Barrett lovingly shared (in front of God, Van, and my parents) that each night before I went to bed I blew a kiss in every direction, just to make sure it reached Van's house. I politely retaliated two weeks later, when Barrett brought home a new girlfriend and I strategically placed a pair of his skid-marked underwear in the middle of his bed.

I guess I figured that since Van knew what a dorky, kid-sister crush I had on him, I had no chance with the guy. But just because I had mild (i.e., for three weeks or less) boyfriends in eighth grade and freshman year, that didn't mean my crush had to stop. That would be like me stopping from fantasizing about making out with Rupert Grint just because I had real make-out sessions with real people, not imaginary, movie-character-wizard ones. I know that. And so does Bizza. And just because I don't talk about Van twenty-four hours a day anymore (although I do still secretly practice late-night Van-directional kissing), one would think that my improbable but still obvious devotion to Van would prevent someone—someone who has called herself my best friend since first grade—from hooking up with him. Perhaps the memory was hidden away in a lock of her hair that is now in the garbage somewhere, because Bizza is not acting the least bit remorseful. In fact, she's going on and on about the whole damn thing.

"I totally made the first move. You inspired me, Jessie, with the Kevin Blane Affair." The Kevin Blane Affair is what Bizza, Char, and I call a blistering summer romance I had with my next-door neighbor's cousin who was visiting from Texas for two weeks before our freshman year. Maybe it was that dream I had about him the day we met (my subconscious has an annoying way of planting boys in my dreams), but something about the whole boy-next-door thing mixed with the impermanence of it made me turn all gutsy. Kevin and I snuck out every night just to make out in the hammock they had in their backyard. And I was the one who started the whole thing by making up some excuse for us meeting in the middle of the night, like "I hear there's going to be a meteor shower tonight." I can be very seductive with science. Thank god he left after two weeks because my lips were getting chapped, I never got enough sleep, and, truthfully, he was a pretty bad kisser.

Ironic, then, that my impulsive make-out saga inspired Bizza to have her very own make-out saga with my very own crush! Couldn't she have been inspired by my sewing or good grades instead? Is she trying to emphasize that I should be over Van anyway since I had a make-out saga with another guy? Is that why she brought the Kevin Blane Affair up? I bet Van's a way-better kisser than Kevin (my fantasies have him right up there with Rupert Grint–quality kissing, and Van's not even a wizard), not that I'll give Bizza the satisfaction of my asking.

"I wonder when we'll hook up again. It was so incredible. Not much room in the front seat. Maybe next time we can move to the back." So glad I don't even have to ask.

"You barely know the guy. No need to move to the back-seat just yet. But before you do, you may want to disinfect." I know I'm just being snarky out of jealousy. If Van had asked me to head to his backseat, I doubt if I'd be pulling out the disinfectant wipes. I'd like to disinfect Bizza's annoying head right now.

"I know he's been with a lot of girls. But he's so hot. And he's a drummer. I really want him to like me."

Just like that, I feel a wee bit empathetic for Bizza. I have never heard her say anything like that. Either people like her or she couldn't care less if they do. The good friend in me even hopes for a second that Van genuinely likes her. I can almost forget the totally new and far-from-improved Bizza 3.0. "Let's make kiddie cocktails," she says. "I could use a stiff one."

I know I should say something about Van and how he's mine, even though he's not mine. But I puss out.

"Coming right up," I say, and like the good friend I am, I make her a drink. Like the friend she is, she lets me.

chapter 8

OUT OF CURIOSITY, I EAT MY LUNCH
on the same bench as I did yesterday. I try to trick myself into
believing that I am eating outside because a) it is so beautiful
out, I might as well take advantage before winter freezes me
back inside and b) I have no one else to eat with. Obviously,
the actual reason is c) to see if Van invites me out to lunch
again.

I almost manage to get involved in my audiobook when
just like out of one of my many Van-tasies (but more probably
out of auto shop) emerges Van. I think he's wearing the same
clothes as yesterday (old black jeans marked with fluorescent
green duct tape and a Bad Brains T-shirt), but it doesn't look
gross. Which is weird, because I remember in fifth grade when
I had this pair of sparkly leggings and a pink button-down to
match (covered in sequined cowboys); I loved them so much I
wore them every single day. Then some skag told me what a
loser I was and how I totally reeked, which was a lie because I
carefully washed them every night when I got home. I tried to
tell her, but she had already moved on to making some other

pathetic tween's life miserable. The moral of this story is: I don't care what Van is wearing (he could even be wearing my leggings-and-cowboy ensemble), he'd still be fine. Admittedly, today he's kind of a cloudy version of Van hot, thanks to the vision of Bizza attached to his face that keeps floating into my brain.

Van looks down at me on the bench and starts talking before I can turn down my audiobook (oblivious to the white cords hanging from my head). "Huh?" I ask him to repeat.

"What are you jamming to?" he asks.

I know he thinks I'm into his music because I use his drum kit, and I don't want him to think I'm a loser because I wasn't actually listening to music in the first place, so I make up, "Oh, some obscure Norwegian band."

"Cool. Cool. So, you ready for lunch?" I love how he ignores my empty lunch bag and just assumes. If Van thinks it's time for lunch, then it's time for lunch.

The scene plays out like a rerun of yesterday—loud music, $2.00 Frosty, and cigarettes. With Van wearing the same outfit, the only difference is my adorable fruit medley skirt, complete with matching vintage fruit bead necklace. "Is that scratch and sniff?" Van points to my skirt after we park back at school. I picture him scratching and sniffing the thin fabric so close to my skin and I get googley.

It's hard to stay mad at him (not that he had any inkling I was mad in the first place) when he's being sort of charming.

44

"Sort of charming" for Van pretty much means he's talking to me. "I think it's just a normal skirt," I manage to say. I turn my face toward his. He really is beautiful up close (if I ignore the stale cigarette smell). His crooked nose, relaxed gray-blue eyes, pillowy lips . . . This totally could have been our second date, and I could maybe have gathered up the nerve to kiss him or let him kiss me. (Why isn't he kissing me, anyway? I wonder if Barrett threatened him. I'll ask Barrett when I get home. And then I'll kill him.) But it doesn't matter because Bizza got there first. Like everything else in our lives, it's all about Bizza. Like that time in eighth grade when our "beloved" English teacher, Mrs. Grossman, decided that Bizza and I should write clever introductions to all of the student council election speeches. (I say "beloved" in quotes because really she was Bizza's beloved English teacher. Not that she wasn't my teacher, but I always got the feeling that she couldn't remember my name. Perhaps it was because she always called me "Jenny.") Like, "You remember him from his crazy science fair project. Don't get too close—he may still be electrified! Give it up for Bill Klein!" Lame, I know, but it was a prestigious gig. Each day after school, Bizza and I set up a video camera and improvised hilarious one-liners and cleverly disguised disses for the candidates. Then, during election week, I got strep and missed the final speeches. According to Polly from my English class, Mrs. Grossman announced in front of the entire school how, and I quote, "I am pleased and proud to let everyone know that every single humorous candidate introduction was written by our very own Bizza Brickman. Stand up, Bizza."

Grrrr. Stand up, Bizza, and steal *my* jokes and *my* cleverness and *my* gorgeous crush. At this moment, blood boiling from the stealing memory, I almost dive into Van's arms for some serious make-out revenge.

But then the bell rings and snaps me out of it. Plus, I could never do it. "I have to get to class," I say, defeated.

"I guess I should, too." Van smiles slyly. What is his deal? I pretend not to notice as he helps me with the sticky door handle. I attempt to coolly speed-walk through the parking lot until I know I'm out of Van's sight, then I sprint to my locker.

Luckily, Mr. Bowles's big stomach is up against the chalkboard as he scribbles equations, so he doesn't notice as I slide into my seat late.

Mike Eastman loudly sniffs the air and leans toward me. "Were you smoking?" He asks so accusingly that I feel the need to lie.

"Yesss," I hiss at him. I'm just so pissed, at myself for being a wuss and at Bizza for being a traitorous bitch. Eventually the logic of math calms me down, and I try to imagine what Bizza is actually thinking about this Van thing. Maybe she really, truly believes that it doesn't matter because it's been my forever crush and if something were to happen, it would have happened already. Or maybe she thinks it doesn't matter because I have technically had more boyfriends than she has. Or perhaps it's that Bizza thinks I'm not even that interested because if I truly liked Van, I would have been at Denny's every night pleading my case. So maybe it's actually all my fault that Bizza hooked up with Van, and I have no reason to be mad.

Or maybe Bizza's kind of a shitty friend.

chapter 9

STUDY HALL IS MUCH QUIETER ON
the second day of school when everyone else has homework.
It's the time of the year when people still have hope that they
can do a good job, keep up with their reading, make the parents proud. Next week a lot of them will already have given
up, realizing it's a lot easier if they just don't do the work. But
not me.

I pull out a short story for English called "Singing My
Sister Down" by Margo Lanagan and try to concentrate, but I
have read the same sentence about ten times, although if you
ask me what the sentence says, I couldn't repeat it. My head is
in the Van clouds (which are more of a cigarette haze than a
cloud).

"You're in that place again. In your head with that guy,
aren't you?" The wise and intuitive Dottie brings me back to
study hall.

"I need a better poker face, don't I?"

"As long as you don't start making out with your hand,
you're fine."

"Oh god. If I ever even look like I *might* do that, please smack me."

"With pleasure." Dottie nods. She goes back to writing something.

"Are you writing in your language again?" I ask, hoping she'll explain what it was she said to me yesterday. I didn't exactly try to figure it out, but I'm still intrigued. It's pretty crazy that someone actually took the time to create and memorize their own language. Although some would say it's crazy that I take the time to make a skirt for every day of the school year.

"No," Dottie answers. I may never learn the mystery of her cryptic good-bye. "I'm working on an adventure."

"I didn't know you wrote stories."

"I don't. It's an adventure. For Dungeons and Dragons."

I look at her blankly.

"Dungeons and Dragons. It's a role-playing game. With dice."

"Ooh—role-playing." I wiggle my eyebrows with innuendo.

"Not that kind of role-playing, perv. It's kind of like *The Lord of the Rings*, but you're the characters."

"So you climb mountains in search of a ring and live in a round house and have hairy feet?" I ask.

She sighs, annoyed. "It's a game. I'm the Dungeon Master, which is like the storyteller, and we sit around a table—a normal table in a normal house—and everyone is a made-up character. I tell a story that the characters are in, like 'You are all in a town, and you're having some mead in the Rusty Skupper Pub, when a frazzled gnome comes over and tells you—"

"A garden gnome? Is he plastic?" I ask dumbly.

"No, duh, like a tiny person. A gnome is one of the races in D&D. Like you're not Caucasian or African-American, you're gnome or elf or human, depending on what you choose. Anyway—the gnome's family has been kidnapped by a band of orcs—"

"What kind of a band? Country? Hip-hop?" I'm pretty much joking just to annoy her at this point.

"Funny. A *group* of orcs. The gnome says he'll pay you if you can get his family back. What do you want to do?"

There's a long pause, and I realize that she's not just explaining the game; she's actually asking me what I would do. "Uh—run around screaming because there's a gnome talking to me about orcs, and I don't even know the guy. And what is mead, anyway?"

She sighs, obviously annoyed by my ignorance. "Forget it. You have to play to really understand. It's totally fun. Takes you away from the real world for a while." When she says that, the game almost sounds appealing. Almost.

"Sounds pretty complicated," I say, not wanting to offend her. "Maybe you can teach me some other time."

She shrugs and goes back to her writing.

I look at Dottie and think about how everyone's got their

"thing." Van and Barrett have the band, Bizza's got her amazing confidence and pseudo-punk thing going on, Char's got her beauty (that's a thing, right?), and even Dottie Bell has a thing—albeit her own language and leading around gnomes. Then there's me. I guess sewing could be my thing, but no one thinks it's very cool. I wish I didn't care.

I try to concentrate on my English reading, and manage to almost finish the story by the time the bell rings. It's so good and frightening, I debate finishing and arriving late to history. I don't, though, because I can finish it *during* history.

Barrett meets me at my locker after school. "No band practice today. Pete's tutoring some fifth grader for extra money. Do you need a ride, or are you hanging with Buzza?" "Buzza" is Barrett's new name for Bizza. I secretly love that he's making fun of her but hate that he put in the effort to give her a nickname.

"I don't really know." I hesitate. Did Barrett know about Van? Bizza and Van? Me and Van? (Not that there's really a me and Van.) I kind of want to talk to Barrett about it, get the guy perspective, but that would mean having to delve back into the humiliation of liking my big brother's friend. Not to mention the insult of Van choosing Bizza over me. Never mind. "Let me get my books and we can go. Bizza didn't say anything about hanging out today." I try to be subtle. "She may be busy." My eyebrows try to get Barrett to understand my hidden meaning. If I don't have to bring up Bizza and Van directly, then that means I'm not really thinking about it.

"Your eyebrows are acting weird again. What gives?" So much for the act of brotherly mind reading. I try the less subtle approach.

"Do you know where Bizza is?"

"Nope. And I can't say I care."

Not helpful. "I just thought you might know since Bizza made Van late to practice yesterday, and I thought he might have mentioned something."

"Van was late to practice because his shitmobile broke down again. Bizza just happened to be his carpool buddy. Are you going somewhere else with this?" Barrett jingles his car keys and looks out the hall windows impatiently, oblivious to my trauma.

Brothers can be such morons. "Nah. I guess I just thought you might know where she is, seeing as she's so tight with your posse."

At that moment Char runs quickly past us in the hall, skids to a stop, and backs up. "Hey, Jess, Barrett." Char looks effortlessly beautiful with her striped hair piled on top of her head in a perfectly messy mound. Her armful of bracelets jangle as she speaks. "I have to get home to watch the demonic twins. Van's giving me a ride. See ya!" She jangles away.

Barrett cracks a grin. "Van's giving her a ride, eh? Looks like he's riding with all your friends, Jessie."

"Yeah, Barrett, and not just in the literal sense." I pause expectantly.

"Meaning?" He shakes his head, disgusted. "Your friends are too young to be hooking up with my friends."

"Barrett, wake up. Bizza and Van were late yesterday because they were screwing around. And don't tell me you haven't thought about Char . . ."

"I only had that dream about her once. I should not have told you." He shuffles his feet, then abruptly goes back to my deal. "Are you sure about Bizza and Van?"

"Pretty sure," I say, sounding more dejected than I'd like.

"He knows you like him. I razz him about it all the time. What a dick." Barrett's face looks pissed, grossed out, and cringy uncomfortable at the same time. "Maybe he needs his ass kicked."

"While I appreciate the sweet gesture of brotherly violence, don't bother. He obviously likes Bizza and not me."

"Those two chodes deserve each other. I hope the STDs flow."

"Um, ick? I'd rather not have to think about anything flowing between Bizza and Van, thank you very much."

We both hang our tongues out at the thought.

"Do you think he's really just giving Char a ride?" I ask.

"Let's hope so, Atreyu. Let's hope so." He quotes our fave kids' movie, *The Neverending Story*, and I'm so grateful he's my brother. And so sad that he'll be gone next year.

chapter 10

TO AVOID ALL CAR GROPING OR ANY
other confusing Bizza interactions, I stay after school to finish
my homework in the library. This also cuts down on back-
breaking textbook hauling. I adopt a "don't ask" policy about
Bizza and Van, and since I don't get to hang (or not hang, as
the case may be) with Bizza after school, avoid her phone
calls, and refuse to turn on my IM when I get home, I'm pretty
much Bizza- and Van-free.

By Friday I've managed maximum avoidance. In English
class, Ms. Norton gives us silent reading time. I have the Fridays, that antsy, can't-wait-to-be-anywhere-but-this-tiny-desk
feeling, and so does Polly. She scribbles notes to me in the
corner of her book.

Polly: I'm so stoked. Jake is coming to visit for the
    weekend.
Me: Is he staying with you?
Polly: In the guest room. My parents are going to a party in
    Wisconsin on Sunday, so they'll be gone for hours!
Me: Sounds fun.

I try not to picture the fun in my head as I'm reminded of what Jake looks like by the photo collage on Polly's binder. Not that I ever really try and picture my friends hooking up, but it's somehow easier when both parties are of the easy-on-the-eyes variety. Crap. Now I actually get why all movie stars have to be unobtainably and unnaturally gorgeous, or no one would want to watch them.

Polly: You?
Me: Not much. Sew some skirts. Listen to book. Homework.

I don't mention that I will be praying that I am somehow magically transported back in time, and I can somehow manage to change the course of history so that Bizza and Char do not, I repeat DO NOT, turn into overnight punks. Maybe I can convince them to join the chess club. Then no one could ever possibly think they're cooler than me. Or at least someone might notice me standing behind them.

In study hall I sit down next to Dottie and smile. "Hey," I greet her.

"You're here," she says. "Not *there*." She wiggles her fingers dreamily.

"*There* isn't the best place for me to be. Actually, I don't know if I ever really was there." I shrug and change the subject. "That's cool. What is it?" I point at a funky wire-and-bead necklace Dottie's wearing.

"It's a twenty-sided die. You know, for role-playing," and I realize that the colorful stone surrounded by wire is actually a die covered in swirling pastels.

"That's really pretty."

"Doug gave it to me after our first date."

"Really? That's sweet. What did you do for your first date?"

"Well, we played D&D at his friend's house. Not very romantic."

"I guess it is if you're into that sort of thing."

"No. It really isn't. He thought it made him look cool in front of his posse, bringing a chick to D&D, seeing as there are never any girls there. Hey—you know what would be rad?" I know what my answer to that question is, but I highly doubt Dottie is thinking the same thing. "If you would come play D&D with us. I would love it if there were another girl there. You interested? We've got a game going tonight."

I know I have the frozen panic look on my face, but I try to shake it off and act casual. "Sorry, I have plans," I lie.

"Maybe another time. We always have room for another player."

"I'll keep that in mind," I say. I pretend to read from my history textbook, but for some reason I'm totally freaked. Talking with Dottie in study hall isn't bad, or saying hi to her in the halls, but hanging out with her on the weekend? That's crossing over into a territory I am not prepared to go. I can't imagine what Bizza would say if she asked what I was doing this weekend (no doubt so she could use me and my brotherly connections for some guaranteed Van time) and I was all, "Oh, you know, fighting some dwarves with Dottie Bell." Nope. Definitely not ready for that.

On my way back from tenth period I catch Barrett and Van talking near my locker. Van looks particularly amazing today, which makes no sense since he's still wearing the same outfit. I think it's the way his hair covers his face just enough to make him look sensitive, but his crooked nose still gives him a little danger. That, and as I watch his lips move while he talks to Barrett I keep fantasizing about him throwing me up against a locker and kissing me (as long as I can keep the image of he and Bizza out of the way). Of all the days for me to wear my Pikachu skirt, which I thought was funny at the time I made it but now think it just looks goofy and babyish.

"Hey, Jess." Barrett catches my arm. He hasn't been keeping up with his Mohawk, and the sides are getting fuzzy, the orange streaky and pale. "Do you mind hitching a ride with Van today? I kind of have an elsewhere to be."

After our previous Van driving conversations, I'm surprised that Barrett will allow me near Van and his car. "Where?" I ask.

"I'm thinking of getting a job at the movie theater. You

know, extra money toward college? Chloe Romano said she could probably get me a job." He mumbles the name, but I hear it clearly.

"Chloe Romano the prom princess?" I laugh.

"That's her," he says, trying to sound dismissive, but definitely trying too hard. I had no idea my brother even knew the prom princess. Maybe they have some classes together or something.

"Okay. Sure. I can go with Van. Good luck with the job thing." Barrett squeezes my arm and does some dorky hand thing with Van that the Crudhoppers made up.

Van watches Barrett walk off, and I watch Van. I fight hard and lose against his bad-boy syndrome.

Van saunters over to me and pinches the hem of my skirt. "Cute," he says, and looks up at my face. Does he have to be such a flirt? If this were any other guy, touching my skirt, smiling his sexy smile at me, it would be so obvious what he wants. But Van—I don't get him. I am so flustered by his attention that I just bust out, "So what's up with you and Bizza?" He lets go of my skirt.

"Nothing really. She's okay. A little young." Strike one for me. "She sure likes me, huh?" And he smacks my shoulder like all of a sudden we're buddies who get stoned every day together outside shop class. He seriously wants me to answer that?

"Yeah, I guess," I try to say with disinterest. Even though I started this convo in the first place.

He leans forward again to finger the hem of my skirt, his thumb rubbing a tiny Pikachu face. "Careful. They bite," I snap, totally disturbed by his simultaneous acts of flirting, bragging, and buddy smacking.

"Oh," he drawls, and my skirt slowly drops from his fingers. Is he stoned? Is that it? Is he so totally high that he thinks it's okay to blow off my too-young friend—even though, technically, she shouldn't like him anyway because he was my crush first—and then touch my Pokèmon skirt? Twice?

"Can you take me home now?" My demanding impatience might make me seem like the Uptight Math Lover (which I kind of am), but the sleaze has hit the fan and I want out.

Van grabs for my hand (what?), and for a second I let him hold it. Haven't I dreamt about moments exactly like this (and beyond) for years? But I'm just way too confused, and I let go with a juvenile giggle. Was he just holding my hand because I'm young and he wants to protect me? Or was he holding my hand to lead me into his den of backseat infestation?

My head spins with questions, and I'm grateful for the lack of AC in his car. Windows down, music blasting, I lean my head out of the window. Curiously, I still see the girl with the straight brown hair in the side-view mirror. How can I look so much the same when everything is happening around me?

When we get to my house, I jam the Gremlin's sticky door open and quickly jump out. As I speed-walk to my front door, Van calls out the passenger window, "Tell Barrett the party's on at my house Sunday. Nine o'clock. You should come, too."

I turn around to catch him wink at me before his car sluggishly pulls away. I have no response because I have no clue what to think or say anymore when it comes to Van.

Inside our house, my dad is in the kitchen washing dishes. "Hi, Jess. How was your official first week back?" he asks.

"Same ol'," I say, just making conversation.

"Bizza called. She told me to tell you she just left you some messages on your cell phone."

I pull my phone out of my backpack. Six missed calls and three messages. I must not have heard it ring over the din in Van's car. Reluctantly, I hit the PLAY MESSAGES button. The first message is from Bizza.

"Hey, Jess, I was thinking we should totally have a good old-fashioned sleepover with Char tomorrow night. Wouldn't that be fun? Kiddie cocktails and sappy movies and shit? We can do each other's hair—just kidding. But yeah, let me know when we should come over to your house. It'll be fun. Later." It's nothing new for Bizza to invite herself to my house on a weekend (she hates when her parents are around), but it's been forever since we had a sleepover. I love the idea, though, and hope it can be like old times. As long as the conversation doesn't turn to Van. Or hair. Or Van's hair.

Char's message is a semi-repeat of Bizza's, but with the added politeness of what snacks should she bring.

The third message is Bizza again. "Heeyyy—there's this party at Van's that we should totally go to on Sunday. I think he'd be cool if you came. Maybe you could ask Barrett to drive us? Cool. Later." Bizza *would* think this was her invite and I'm just tagging along. Um, he asked me, thank you very much. With a wink, no less. But of course my brother will drive us. How frigging annoying, yet so Bizza. Then I remember how Van said *she* liked *him* and not the other way around, and I feel a little better. But also a little bitchy.

I return to the kitchen for a snack, and Barrett walks in with a big grin. "You are looking at the newest member of the Greenville Cinema concession stand butter pumpers. I start next week."

"Congrats," I say as I yank on a stalk of celery with my teeth. "Free popcorn for family, right?" I hint.

"I think I can manage to sneak you some day old, if you're good," Barrett teases, grabbing a can of cream soda from the fridge.

"Oh, then I'll be sure to be on my best behavior," I say dryly. "By the way, Van told me to tell you that the party is on Sunday at nine at his house."

"A party? On a Sunday?" Dad cracks eggs into a bowl to make omelets for dinner.

"It's Labor Day, Dad," I tell him.

"How could I forget? America's reward for the poor teachers who had to go back to work." Dad looks out the kitchen window dreamily.

"Can I go?" I ask.

"I don't see why not, as long as you don't stay out too late," Dad answers.

"I was kind of talking to Barrett."

"Ouch." Dad staggers, pretending I stabbed him in the heart. "My little girl doesn't need me anymore."

"Daaaad." I love it when he calls me his little girl. I know it's the type of thing that annoys most people, but for me it means that it's okay if I don't change too much. Definitely dorky.

"Sure you can come. And you'll be bringing the poseurettes, I assume?"

"You assume correctly. In fact, according to Bizza, she's bringing us. With you as chauffeur, of course."

"Good old Buzza," Barrett muses as he helps Dad chop vegetables.

After avoiding Van and Bizza and all of their whatever all week, I get to spend a three-day weekend completely consumed in their whatever. Can't wait.

chapter 11

I'M UP EARLY SATURDAY MORNING,
working on a new skirt. After every holiday the fabric store
has a mega sale on the appropriate fabrics, so I stock up. I'm
working on a series of valentine skirts, and I have enough different sale fabrics from last year to last almost the entire month
of February (a nice short month). This particular skirt is filled
with goofy Dalmatians and hearts on a red background. So
random.

I called Bizza and Char last night and okayed the sleepover. My parents are always happy to host, and since they are
both teachers all day, they've seen enough children during the
week and usually stay out of our way.

As I sew, I listen to an audiobook. This one is called *Life
as We Knew It*, about a teenage girl trying to survive with her
family after a meteor hits the moon, pushing it closer to Earth.
Because the moon affects the tides, there are tsunamis and
earthquakes everywhere. The possibility of this actually happening is scaring the crap out of me. Way more than the Stephen King.

I'm almost finished with the skirt when Barrett groggily

walks by my open bedroom door. "Morning, Sunshine." He yawns.

I hold up my skirt, and he gives it a logy thumbs-up as he makes his way to the bathroom. I go on sewing, freaking as I listen to the world possibly coming to an end. The shortage of food is making me really hungry.

Barrett, Mom, and I eat a breakfast of Dunkin' Donuts, our Saturday morning ritual. Dad stopped participating a couple of years ago after the doctor told him his cholesterol was high. He can't even be in the kitchen with the donuts because, as he put it, "That smell haunts me." Right now he's in the garden as we gluttonize.

I pick up one of my two donuts, a strawberry frosted. It is so perfect and smooth, I almost hate to eat it. That feeling lasts for only a second as I bite into the flaky goodness.

"Did you know"—Mom says between bites of a (gross) jelly-filled—"that Dunkin' Donuts used to package their dozens in a different box than this? It was more like a shoe box, six donuts per side. They always stuck together, so even if you just wanted a strawberry glaze you'd end up with a little chocolate on the back or some powered sugar."

"Please tell me not jelly?" I fake panic.

"I'm afraid so, dear. I think that they started laying donuts flat after Krispy Kreme became popular."

We all boo. Our family hates Krispy Kreme. Krispy

Kreme stores were only recently introduced to the Midwest and were a huge deal when they popped up in random cities. We had already been celebrating Dunkin' Donuts since forever, so we were hesitant to give another franchise our business. We drove over forty-five minutes for the grand opening of the nearest Krispy Kreme store, and when we got there it was packed. Line out the door. So we waited. And waited. When we finally got inside, we watched the donuts ride through their shower of whiteness. By the time we got to the counter, we were starving. Like the donut-loving fools we are, we ordered three dozen original glazed because we were just so excited that the warm donut light was on. Plus, whatever we couldn't finish we would share with the neighbors. In the car, I wolfed down two hot, melty donuts. My dad, pre-cholesterol check (perhaps this is what upped his cholesterol to deadly proportions) ate five or six (he ate them so fast, he lost count). My mom had a couple, but sipped her coffee to slow her down. Barrett was the only one who contained himself, and not because he was on a diet. As I gorged, he watched with a disgusted look. "What?" I demanded, my mouth full of creamy donut goo.

"How can you eat them after seeing that stuff dribble down on them on the conveyer belt?"

"You mean that white stuff? The glaze?" I couldn't see a problem.

"It looked like"—he paused for grody, dramatic effect—"jizz."

"Barrett!" my mom yelled from the front seat. My dad stopped eating.

"What's jizz?" I asked, hating to be naive.

"Yes, Barrett, why don't you tell your little sister what jizz is, since you brought it up?"

Barrett looked incredulously at Mom. "You're the parent. You should educate her on such matters."

"If you're going to use a word like *jizz* in my car, young man, *and* ruin my magical donut experience, then you can give the sex-ed lecture," my dad said. He wasn't so much mad as he was annoyed that he had to stop stuffing in the donuts in order to have a conversation.

"Whatever." Barrett turned to me all big brotherly. "You see, Jessie, when a man and a woman love each other—"

"Shut up!" I yelled, embarrassed. "I had sex ed last year, thank you very much, and they didn't say anything about Krispy Kremes. Just get to the point."

"You know that stuff showering down from Krispy Kreme heaven?" Barrett asked me seriously.

"Yeah."

"You know that stuff that shoots out of a guy's . . ." He didn't have to finish, thanks to a graphic diagram that popped into my head from the boy portion of our sex-ed film.

"Ohmigod." I was mortified, not to mention disgusted. Just as Barrett, I'm sure, would never want to know what my period looks like, I had no interest in visualizing his bodily functions.

"Well, now that that's over . . ." Dad closed up the first box of our three dozen. On our way home we stopped at a gas station and left the three flat Krispy Kreme boxes on top of a garbage can. Thus, every Saturday we eat Dunkin' Donuts.

I work on my second donut, always a colored sprinkler. I especially enjoy a holiday-themed colored sprinkler. Today's is just a common multicolored.

"What time are your friends coming over tonight?" Mom asks me.

"Who's coming over?" Barrett asks suspiciously.

"Bizza and Char. Around seven."

"But we have band practice tonight," Barrett practically whines. "I don't want your friends invading the basement to swoon and interrupt with nauseating stories of sophomore rebellion."

"I don't want that either," I say, annoyed, as if it's my fault that my friends chose this new, punkified way of life. "It's not like I want to sit around watching the Crudhoppers suck." I was hitting below the belt, but this adds a whole new cruddy dimension to the evening. Am I going to have to spend the whole night finding new and exciting ways to keep my friends out of the basement?

"Why don't you just put a sign on the door?" my mom suggests. "Like, 'Keep out. Genius at work.' " I laugh at my mom's attempt at intervention.

"Mom, you know Bizza. Even if the sign spelled out in giant, hot pink letters, 'Keep out, Bizza,' she would just turn it around in some way. Like, 'It says my name, so they must actually want me down there.' She doesn't take no, and she doesn't think it's possible for someone to not want her around." I slump.

"Jessie, there's a lot going on with the 'Hoppers right now. Can you please try to keep the punk-lites out of the basement?" Barrett uses his puppy-dog eyes on me, and he did say *please*.

"I'll try," I say. Now I just have to think of 10,000 things for us to do in order to keep Bizza and Char from descending into forbidden territory.

I'm so edgy about tonight that I frantically make three more skirts. This audiobook doesn't help. The family is almost out of food, and the air is dark and freezing and there's no one around to help. I must remember to ask my mom about what canned goods we have stored in our pantry.

When the book is finally over (with a slightly relieving ending, although not enough to take the edge off), I lay down on my bed to work on my precalc homework. Nothing like math to make me forget about everything for a while. I make it through about three problems before I decide to straighten up my room for my impending guests. The doorbell rings as I finish clearing off my bedroom floor to make room for Bizza's and Char's sleeping bags. I hear my mom open the door, and soon Bizza and Char are clomping up the stairs in their giant boots.

"Hey girl." Bizza throws her stuff into a corner of my room. Her outfit is new to me: weird, kiltlike skirt, "vintage" Sex Pistols T-shirt, and these boot-shoe combination things with metal buckles. Char's long hair is divided into dozens of multicolored braids. She's wearing what I guess is a dress, but it looks more like a Victoria's Secret nightie, finished off with her jumbo combat boots.

"Take off your shoes and make yourself comfortable," I say, dreading the thought of listening to the clomping all night.

"Maybe later," Bizza says, and she sits on the rug, legs crossed. I don't see how that can be comfortable with those hard boots under her legs.

I walk over to Char and feel her braids. "You like? I did it while I was babysitting last night. Actually, the twins helped. I taught them how to braid and then made it into a contest to see who could make the most braids the fastest. I thought they would pull off my head, but they did a pretty good job. Now I have to bake them chocolate chip cookies, but I would do that anyway. Speaking of . . ." Char pulled a Tupperware container out of her bag.

"Pecan tassies!" Bizza and I shout at the same time. Char's a fantastic baker, probably because she's forced to spend so many hours at home. Pecan tassies are beautiful, my favorite, like tiny little pecan pies. She bakes them for us only on special occasions.

"Thank you, thank you, thank you!" I hug Char and grab the container from her hands. Opening the lid, I inhale the pecan-y goodness. "May I?" I ask, tassie already so close to my mouth that no one else would want to eat it, anyway.

"Of course. I made them for you. But don't eat too many. I want to give some to the Crudhoppers when they get here."

A sound goes through my head like a car slamming on its brakes and skidding forty feet. Of course they knew the Crudhoppers were coming over. Why else would they want to be here? God forbid it be to enjoy *my* company.

There is no way of keeping them out of the basement now. So much for my nostalgic sleepover. Shit.

chapter 12

MY EXPECTATIONS OF RELIVING OUR
joyous youth fizzles with every application of Bizza's extra-
black eyeliner. I don't know how I could have thought that
things could go back to stupid movies, karaoke, and Ouija
board sessions. We're big girls now, and anything social must
involve boys. Girl power be damned.

"I think I OD'd on tassies." I excuse myself as if to go to
the bathroom, and then creep down the stairs toward the basement. As I open the basement door, I hear Barrett on the
phone in the kitchen.

"Yeah, we have practice tonight. But if it doesn't go too
late, maybe we can hook up." He notices me, and he shifts his
position to hide his words. "I gotta go. Talk to you later." He
laughs. "Me, too." He hangs up quickly and says to me, "Hey,
why aren't you upstairs with your friends?"

"Whatever. Who was on the phone? And don't say no one
because it was obviously someone. And most definitely a
girl."

"Nancy Drew's got nothing on you, Jessie. I don't know
how you figured it out, seeing as you had a fifty percent chance

of getting the gender right." Barrett is so trying to cover something up.

"No need to be a butt. Who was it?"

"A girl. Someone from school. From work. Uh, that girl Chloe."

Total avoidance of eye contact. Barrett picks at a hangnail.

"Chloe Romano?" Chloe Romano has one of those names that you have to say in entirety every time, partially to differentiate her from the million other Chloes at our school, but mostly because she is not one of those people you ever get to know in any sort of personal way. She's more abstract prom princess/honors student/all-around-gorgeous, plastic, generic teen. So why is my brother getting his boxers in a bundle about her?

"Chloe Romano," he answers as a yes. "She helped me get my job at the theater. And we might be going out sometime." He opens and closes random drawers in an effort to distract me.

"Excuse me?"

"Please don't make me say it again." He's got his back to me, drawers now shut.

"What could be so bad, Barrett? It's not like you're going out with the prom princess."

He turns around with a "Surprise!" grin.

"No way!" My eyes bulge. "Chloe Romano? And my punk rock, Mohawked brother? You're shitting me."

"Keep your voice down." He moves closer to me so he can talk at a near whisper. "The 'Hoppers are gonna be here soon. And I don't want anyone to know. It's not exactly cool for me to be going out with the prom princess."

"No kidding. How did it . . . *happen?*" I punctuate the word like I'm touching dirty underwear.

"I don't know. We had a class together. Shared some notes. She said she could get me a job at the movie theater. She was in my car. She smelled really good and had on an incredibly short skirt and . . ."

"TMI, Barrett. So you like her?"

"Yeah, I guess. I mean yes. I like her," he admits with a sheepish grin.

"And she likes you?" Not that I would doubt that anyone could like Barrett. He is any girl's dream. I just never thought of the prom princess as any girl.

"Hey. *She* called *me*. Is that so hard to believe?" He's defensive, but I can tell he wants me to be okay with this.

"No. I mean, not from her side, but I didn't know you liked girls like that. You always dated the freaksters before."

"Well, maybe I'm tired of getting punctured by lip rings and trying to outcool each other. Chloe doesn't care about any of that."

"And she does have those legs." I laugh.

Barrett waggles his eyebrows up and down. "So don't tell anyone, okay? Let me figure out what it is first."

"Okay. But if she starts coming over here and tries to teach me a cheer or some other crap, I can't promise anything."

"Cool. So why are you down here and not upstairs with your gal pals?" He relaxes and regains normal volume.

What am I going to do when Barrett goes off to college? He's always so good at taking my mind off my stupid life when we talk about his. "They're"—I pause guiltily—"getting ready for the Crudhoppers' practice."

"Jessie!"

"I didn't say anything! They already knew!" I moan.

"See, this is what I'm talking about. This 'scene.' What kind of band are we if we can't even play music? I'm so glad I got the job at the theater." He hoists himself onto the kitchen counter. "It's totally gonna be my excuse."

"Excuse for what?"

"To get out of the band."

I gasp. The Crudhoppers have always been part of my tween-to-teen existence. They're what gave me an in to the cool punk scene at school, not that I really wanted it, but it was a good thing to have. I practiced with them or watched them practice or went to their shows. They were my biggest excuse for seeing Van. Without Barrett in the band, I have zero coolness connections. I refuse to count Bizza and Char. I want to tell Barrett how this will affect me, but what can I say? This is Barrett's thing, and I'm just the tagalong kid sis. Now that Bizza and Char are with the band, so to speak, they won't care if Barrett's out. I'm sure they can get plenty of rides from Van. With or without me.

The Crudhoppers' practice is as I expected. Between every song is a lot of yammering and jabbering (old-lady speak for "talking out of one's ass") from Bizza and Char. A second ago, Van hopped off his drums, sat on our groovalicious basement couch, and patted the seats next to him for Bizza and Char to join him.

"Are we practicing or what?" Barrett has no patience and gives me a "see?" look. Not wanting to look at the couch activities, I fill in for Van on drums for what may be my last time, once Barrett makes his announcement. I count out the beats and do a decent job keeping up, trying to keep my focus on the music and not my guy-crazy friends.

At around 11:30, Doc Mom peeks her head in and swirls her finger in the air—her sign for "It's time to wrap it up because your dad and I are going to bed." There is also the two hands waving frantically, which means "the neighbors have complained and threatened to call the police."

After ten minutes of the clanging and buzzing of putting away the instruments, Van finally notices. "What? Practice over already?"

"Practice? You played two songs." Barrett is angry, but I can tell he's acting angrier than he really is. He clenches his fists, which he never does, for buildup. I think this is it.

"I know them fine." Van waves Barrett off. "Don't freak out, man." The other Crudhoppers stop what they are doing. What's the guy version of a catfight?

"You don't know shit, *Van*." Barrett's emphasis mocks the absurd coolness of Van's name. "My kid sister plays better than you, and she's played drums half as long as you have." Why does he have to drag me into this? I couldn't be further than I am right now from being one of Van's hoochies. "You don't take this band seriously," Barrett continues, with his fists clenched tightly, "and you never will." Eric and Pete nod in agreement.

"Then maybe your kid sister can fill in for me permanently." It hurts having Van refer to me as a kid sister. From Barrett, it's a protective term of endearment. From Van, it just makes me young and anonymous.

Pleading cries of "No! You're so good!" come from Bizza and Char. I wonder if they're so upset because they really want Van to stay in the band or because they really don't want *me* to be in it.

"I have a better idea." Barrett states this like he just thought of it. "Why don't you stay and play your half-assed drums, and *I'll* leave the band?"

Eric and Pete plead, "Come on, man," and "We can work this out," but through Barrett's anger I can already see relief.

"I'm out of here," Van declares. "Are you girls coming?" He stomps up the basement steps without waiting for Bizza's and Char's answers. I know his "girls" don't include me.

"Jessie." Bizza steps up to me, and I believe almost for a moment that she'll do the right thing and continue on with our sham of a sleepover. All the harder the slap in my face when she says, "Will you let us in when we get back? We won't be gone that long."

What am I supposed to say? "Young ladies! While you are guests in my house you will abide by my rules. No smoking, drinking, or spitting. And absolutely no leaving the house at midnight to go off with some guy ho who I still have an un-explainable crush on!" Of course I actually say, "I guess. But if you're not back by two, I'm going upstairs to bed and you can just sleep outside." I try to be tough, but Bizza gives me a giant squeeze. "Thanks, Jess. We owe you." I can only imagine what currency Bizza thinks she can pay me back with—betrayal? Annoyance? How about complete and utter lack of respect? She's rich with that.

I flop down on the basement couch and watch Barrett say good-bye to Eric and Pete. "Sorry, guys," he says. "It hasn't been working for a long time."

"The 'Hoppers won't be the same without you, man." Eric's handshake with Barrett turns into a backslap hug. Do guys think this makes them look more manly?

"Yeah, man, I mean, where will we practice?" Pete smacks Barrett's back and gives him the 'Hoppers secret shake.

"Later."

Barrett sinks down next to me on the couch. "I guess it's just you and me, Jess," he says, shutting his eyes. I know he means right here at this moment it's just the two of us, but I can't help but feel like maybe Barrett's all that's left. Have I lost my two best friends to punk? And what about when Barrett leaves for college? Will it be just me?

I fall asleep on Barrett's shoulder until I hear giggly knocking coming from the outside door that leads into the kitchen. I take the stairs two at a time so they don't wake up my parents.

Bizza and Char reek of cigarette smoke, and they barely notice when I open the door for them without speaking. I walk upstairs to my bedroom, and they quietly follow until we're all inside and the door is closed. Silently, I put on a T-shirt and climb into bed. I roll into a ball, pull the blanket over my head, and face the wall.

"Jess," Bizza whisper-yells. "We had so much fun!"

"You can tell me about it tomorrow. Go to bed."

I drift off to their inaudible whispers and shuffling sleeping bags. When I wake up early Sunday morning, they are both sound asleep. I look at Bizza and Char and remember the countless sleepovers together, when we used to set up haunted houses and puppet shows, Barbie beauty pageants and couch forts. Next to them now are piles of black clothes, heavy boots, and mall punk accessories. Even though we slept together in the same room, there isn't an ounce of togetherness left between me and the two of them. I still can't help but wish there were.

chapter 13

WHEN BIZZA AND CHAR FINALLY
wake up, it's already time for lunch. My family plans to go on
a bike ride all afternoon, so I have a good excuse to make them
leave.

As they pack up their stuff, Char says, "Thanks for covering for us last night, Jess. We never could have gotten out if
we stayed at Bizza's house with that jacked-up alarm system
they have."

"No problem," I say, but not in a happy-go-lucky, "no
problem" way. More of a "like I had a choice" way. I'm definitely confused as to how Char even fits into this whole Van
equation. As much attention as she gets from guys, she's always been good about not getting, or at least not acknowledging, attention from *my* guys. And this my guy is now sort of
Bizza's guy, so I doubt she's going along with this for the Van
benefits. But why isn't Char saying anything about how weird
this all is? Still, she baked my favorite treats (not just for me,
but I partook), and she did thank me. These are my best
friends. I can't just dismiss that.

I get no thank-you from Bizza, but instead, "So what time

will Barrett pick us up tonight? How about around eight?" I just love how Bizza can ask a question and give me the answer at the same time.

"I don't know if we're still going. I mean, with the breakup of the Crudhoppers and all." Seeing as the hurt party is my brother, my hesitation should make sense.

"Come on, Jess, it won't be any fun without you." Bizza tries to look all sweet, but who is she kidding? She'll be so busy jonesing for the attention of others that she won't pay any attention to me. Plus, it's really hard to look sweet with a buzz cut and runny eyeliner.

"Please." Char squeezes my hand. Her mystical kindness makes me think that maybe it will be okay. Maybe even fun. And I do have a new skirt I'd like to debut.

"I guess I'll go. But why don't you just get Van to drive? He seems to love driving everyone around."

"We can't ask Van. It's his party. He's got, like, guests and shit to worry about," Bizza says as she ties and buckles her boots.

Guests and shit. How *could* I be so naive? "Okay. We'll come get you around eight, I guess." I say "around" just to give myself a little bit of power. I'll make sure we're at least ten minutes late. Ha!

"You're the best, Jess," Bizza calls absently as she and Char leave.

Barrett walks into my room and mimics, "You're the best, Jess."

"Shut up. You're still driving us to the party, you know."

"Why should I drive you to the party? I'm not even going. They should ask their boy toy." Barrett studies his reflection in my dresser mirror.

"He has 'guests and shit' to worry about," I mock Bizza with a dead-eyed imitation. "Besides, you have to go! I don't want to be alone with those two goobs."

"No can do. I have my very first official date with Chloe tonight." He brushes his mohawk out of his eyes and tries to flatten it against the side of his head.

"Chloe Romano?" I ask, still in denial that my brother is hot for a popular chick.

"Must you ask me that every time I say her name?" He is obviously deliberating some hair decision.

"What are you doing next? Blue? Purple? Pink?"

"I was thinking more like gone."

"Like, all gone?"

"Yep."

"Like, Mom-will-shit-a-brick gone?"

"Yeah, well, it isn't Mom who has to deal with the upkeep. And the cost of hair dye. And the time it takes for me to get ready in the morning if I want the 'hawk to stand up perfectly straight."

I used to think it was so cool and brave for Barrett to have a Mohawk when no one else at school did. Now that Bizza took it one step further, I don't think it's quite as cool. "It's just hair," I say. "Do what you want."

I stand next to him and look at us together in the mirror. Barrett's evolving hair and my straight brown hair. Sometimes I wish I could be as brave as Barrett (and, I hate to admit, Bizza). But most of the time, I think my straight brown sitting-at-the-shoulders, same-as-it's-been-for-the-past-five-years hair is perfect for me. If only everything else could stay the same.

chapter 14

GETTING READY FOR THE PARTY AT Van's is bittersweet. In the past, just the thought of going to Van's house made me tingly—being so near to everything he touched, the possibility of seeing his used laundry somewhere (although, he probably doesn't have much laundry if he always wears the same clothes), and my über-fantasy of him taking me up to his bedroom. Now I have to worry about the possibility of him taking someone else up to his room. I'm not an idiot. I know Van has been with a million girls, but they've all just been anonymous punk chicks with whom I have zero connection. Now the chance that the girl going to his bedroom is my oldest and (gag) dearest friend seems all too real. I can only hope that way back in Bizza's pea brain, she has a spark of recognition that I like Van. I'd say something, but I'm scared that she actually does know and she'd use some of her magical Bizza wiles to make me feel like somehow I'm in the wrong. The most I can hope for is that at the right moment, the memory will magically snap her out of her hoochie state and she'll run down the stairs, away from his lusty lair, and back to her best friend where she belongs.

Yeah, and maybe I'll shave my head today.

My party skirt looks as cute as I thought it would. I found some iridescent reflective fabric, perfect for an alien costume (or a doomed punk party). I love the way it seems to change color depending on what colors are near it, like a chameleon. I slip into some sequined flats (I might as well go sparkly all the way), and knock on the bathroom door to retrieve Barrett. He decided he'd rather drive me than force me to get a ride with some freak (not that that was even an option), and after that he'll head out into unknown, cheerleading waters.

My knock pushes open the door to reveal Barrett leaning over the sink, clippers in hand. All but a tiny tuft of hair above his forehead remains of his once-glorious mohawk.

"Just give me one more second," he says, and *BZZZZ*, the mohawk is gone. "Ta-da!" He holds out jazz hands to display his newly shorn head.

"Back to basics, then?"

"Good for new jobs, college interviews, and dates with prepster hotties."

"Don't go changing just to impress Chloe Romano." I'm disappointed at the thought.

"It's not for her, Jess," he says as he grabs clumps of hair and stuffs them into a grocery bag. "She loves the mohawk. I think she likes the idea that she's going out with some weirdo. But I'm tired of being the weirdo. I'm tired of living up to everyone's expectations of coolness. I'm so over it." He runs the water in the sink to wash away the remaining hairs. "Are you ready to go?"

I nod and feel more alone than ever. My big brother, who I could always count on to make me feel cool by association, has abandoned the punk-rock ship for preppier waters. Tonight I'm invading full-on punk territory, without my big brother and with two girls who no longer resemble my friends. At least my skirt is cute.

Bizza gets into Barrett's car, and I just about throw up. She's not wearing a shirt. All she's got on is some faux-sexy lacy black bra. And I'm not just saying it's a shirt that looks like a bra. She's wearing a friggin' bra. And a kilt.

"You forgot something," I tell her as she plops into the backseat.

"Ha-ha," she retorts. Without hesitation, she rubs Barrett's newly shorn head. "We're twins," she sings merrily.

"Not really," he says. "I'm wearing a shirt."

The funny thing is, and I'm not just saying this to be bitchy (well, maybe a little), Bizza doesn't even look good with her shirt off. It's not that she's sporting a severe kilt muffin top or anything; it's that her bra, sexy or not, is barely, well, filled. One of my greatest triumphs over Bizza is that I at least have an average (to above average when I'm bloated from my period) sized chest. Bizza never developed as much in that area, and her attempt at sexy doesn't work as well as she'd like. I'm trying not to think "score one for Jessie," but it's hard not to when her not-so-ample bosom is staring the world in the face.

We pick up Char, who's decked out in a bizarre tight green jumpsuit (which she completely pulls off), and follow the faint sound of thumping bass until it crescendos at Van's house. "Last Stop: Punker Junction," Barrett announces in his train conductor voice.

"Thanks, B," Bizza says as she slams her way out of the car. Barrett turns to me and mouths, "B?" I shrug and say good-bye to my abandoning brother.

Funky, junked-up cars covered in punk band bumper stickers litter the driveway and street. I walk three steps behind Bizza and Char and consider turning around and chasing Barrett down before he gets too far. Then I see Van standing outside his front door, having a cigarette and greeting people as they arrive. He looks annoyingly beautiful in his native habitat, and he even changed his shirt for the occasion: a vintage tee telling everyone to "Save the Humans."

Bizza and Char arrive at Point Van, and Bizza pulls Van's ear close to her mouth. She whispers something, and he smiles slyly. As she continues her sweet nothings, Van looks directly at me. His smile grows into a friendly, Jessie-melting smile, and he winks. I guess I could stay a few minutes.

Inside is a mix of semifamiliar faces from Crudhoppers' shows mixed with unfamiliar, older faces. Some look way out of high school range, which feels a little cool but also a little lame. (Why would high school graduates want to be at a party with high school students, when they could be drinking somewhere else legally, or even possibly running for president?) I pop a squat on a couch near the "dance floor" (the family room with most of the furniture removed). People are attempting to dance to the mix of punk and reggae and thrash coming from the stereo, but it doesn't quite have that dancing beat. Char thankfully comes and sits down next to me with a frothy beverage in a plastic cup. "You want a beer, Jess? I can get you one. The guy at the keg is superfine."

Tempted, but flashing back to the one time I did drink beer (which I had to drink a lot of to get past the puke/piss taste) and the vomitous aftermath. "No thanks. I'm good."

Char sips and nods to the "beat." Guys pass us and give Char the up-and-down, undressing-her-with-their-eyes look she must be so used to. I get an occasional glance, but I think mostly because people are drawn, like bugs, to my shiny skirt. After about fifteen minutes of this and no sight of Van, I'm over it and ready to go. Char has made casual conversation (which amounts to very few, very loud words to be heard over the blasting music) with about thirty boys of various punk incarnations during this short time. I was particularly impressed with the guy who looked to be about forty, a bull's ring through his nose and the word "Mom" lovingly tattooed on his freakishly large bicep.

"Where's Bizza?" I ask Char between visitors.

"With Van." She gives me some look with her eyes that I know is supposed to mean something I don't even want to think about. "You've been really cool about this whole thing, Jessie. Better than I would be."

"What do you mean?" I assume Char is referring to this crapass party.

"You know, letting Bizza have Van, even though you liked him for practically forever." I feel both relieved that Char is finally acknowledging this and pissed that she didn't bother to try and stop Bizza.

"It's not like I let her *have* him; he chose her."

"Hardly." Char laughs and sips her beer. "Bizza's been stalking the guy all summer. How could he possibly say no? I mean, shit, she's not even wearing a shirt tonight. How much easier can she make things?"

Things. Ick. I cannot think of those things or I might heave all over the floor and some poor, unsuspecting mosher could slip and fall.

With her perfectly assy timing, Bizza appears through the dancing punks. She thuds herself down on the couch in a small space between me and Char. Her bare leg is warm against mine, and I slide over to avoid more contact. "Can I have some of that?" Bizza points to Char's beer. "I need to clear my throat."

"You *didn't?*" Char asks in an excited, naughty way. Bizza just smiles and grabs Char's cup. She chugs it until there's a thin foam left.

"Didn't what?" I hate that they are in on something, again, and I'm the dork trying to figure it out.

"I was upstairs." Bizza turns to me. "With *Van*?" She says this like a question, as if that's supposed to tell me anything. I'm already grossed that Bizza did, in fact, make it to one of my dream destinations, and then she makes things even grosser. "And I needed to clear my throat?" Another question.

But this time I have the repulsive answer.

"You blew Van?"

I don't need to look at her to feel her nod. Thank god I didn't have a beer because I would be full-on blowing chunks right now. It's a combination of a million things—Bizza in Van's bedroom, Bizza and Van period, the blow job. . . . She'd really do that. With Van. Then I remember Barrett and his Krispy Kreme talk, and I almost laugh. It's gross and stupid and so Bizza at the same time. Pathetic. She comes to a party in her bra to blow some guy who she's been stalking all summer. *The* guy. The never-was-but-will-always-be *my* guy. Not that I think I'd do what she did with *my guy*, but I'm speechless that my "best friend" (huge, freakin' finger quotes) would stoop so low. Pun absolutely intended.

The silence annoys Bizza, because she asks, "What's wrong, Jessie? Are you mad?" I want to detect a hint of fear in her voice, but the music is so loud I can't tell.

"Why would I be mad?" is my passive-aggressive answer. Why, after weeks of her lusting after my secret-ish crush, would I be mad?

" 'Cause of me and Van," she says cautiously.

I flip my hand up and scrunch my lips in an "And . . . ?" gesture.

"Well, I know you like him. Or liked him, at least. I thought you might be a little jealous." She's part cautious and part cocky, and I can't stand it. Is she kidding? Of course I'm jealous! And not just of this. I'm jealous that she can get away with looking like an ass-hat but thinking she's so cool. I'm jealous that she gets every bit of attention that someone smarter and funnier and nicer than her—i.e., ME—deserves. And I'm jealous that Bizza can somehow be so oblivious to other people's feelings that she doesn't care how many people she shits on, even her oldest, best friend.

"You know what, Bizza?" I stand up, looking down at her. "You're a bitch."

I storm out of the party and walk until I'm far enough away that I don't hear any more bass. I'm not crying. I'm swearing. Swearing and cursing the crap out of Bizza and her stupid, selfish fuzzy head. When I finally have enough of walking, I pull out my cell phone and call Barrett.

"Can you come get me?" I yell into the phone wildly the second he answers.

"Jess, I'm out with Chloe. What's up?" I swear I hear soft rock playing in the background.

Crap. I forgot about Chloe. "Never mind. I don't want to interrupt." A quick image of Barrett and Chloe in the backseat of his car, pom-poms flying, pops into my head.

"No, it's okay. We can come get you. Are you still at Van's?" I tell him what corner I'm standing on, and he says he'll be here soon. What am I going to do next year when I'm stuck at a party and need a ride home? Call Doc Mom or Dad? Not likely. I can just hear Dad blabbing on about all of the parties he used to go to in high school and how I have to rise above peer pressure and . . . god. I'm boring myself just thinking about it. Thankfully, my ex-besty betrayed me while Barrett's still home. Silver lining, right?

While I wait for my savior, I relive Bizza's final questions to me. Am I mad? Am I jealous? And the worst part of it all, that she knew I liked Van and still did all of this.

A few minutes later, Barrett pulls up with Chloe Romano in the front seat. She really is pretty: shiny black hair, crystal blue eyes, a genuine smile. I climb into the backseat, embarrassed to barge in on their date. Barrett looks back at me, concerned. "Jessie, this is Chloe. Chloe, Jessie."

"Nice to meet you," I say in an obligated, little-kid way.

"Same here." She smiles. "Barrett talks about you all the time." This makes me perk up a bit.

"So can I ask what happened?" Barrett's driving now, away from the scene of the slime.

"As long as you don't freak out on anyone," I warn.

"Why would I freak out?" Barrett says, freaking out. "What happened?" He still wants to believe that any problems I have are about Barbies and Transformers.

"Um, it's kind of gross." I don't know if I should be saying any of this in front of Chloe Romano. "Kind of personal."

"You're not making me any less freaked out by not saying anything, Jess." He sounds like he's trying to keep it together in front of Chloe Romano. He looks at me in the rearview mirror, and I point with my head toward her, like maybe this conversation doesn't need to happen in front of company.

I guess Chloe senses my hesitation because she says, in a surprisingly friendly, easygoing manner, "It's okay. I won't be offended. Or grossed out. And I won't tell anyone. Or I don't even have to listen. No worries."

I really don't want to have to wait, so I take a deep breath and bust out, "Bizza gave Van a blow job even though she knows I like him. Or I *liked* him." The faster I speak, the faster I get the humiliation out of the way.

"Dick!" Barrett yells, then looks over at Chloe Romano. "Sorry," he mutters. Chloe shrugs like she doesn't care. "She's just a kid. No offense, Jess, but shit. He can screw any girl he wants and then he forces my kid sister's friend to suck him off? He's so freaking dead when I see him on Tuesday." The protective-big-brother thing is both comforting and scary.

"I don't think he forced her. I mean, she didn't seem upset."

Chloe responds, "You should ask her what *she* got out of

it. It's one thing to have oral sex with someone you know and trust, but now every girl thinks the way to popularity is through blow jobs. I had this huge talk with my little sister about this. If a guy is only going to like you because you're the girl who says yes to putting his dick in your mouth, then forget him. And why is it always about girls giving something to guys? It's never the other way around, you know? So many double standards."

I'm stunned at how openly Chloe Romano is talking to me about not giving guys blow jobs. I guess there's a part of me that believes that if a girl is gorgeous and superpopular, she must be kind of a ho. What am I supposed to say, though? It's not as though I've ever sat around theorizing on the gender inequalities of oral sex. I guess it makes sense when you think about it, but I haven't really thought about it.

Chloe must notice the foggy look on my face, because she turns around and says, "My mom teaches Women's Studies at UW Madison. She's raised me not to succumb to all of the bullshit pressure society puts on females. I try, anyway."

Barrett looks back at me in the rearview mirror with a smile that says, *Now do you see why I like her?*

Barrett and Chloe drop me off at home, and I wave as I watch them drive off. If Chloe Romano can be a surprise feminist, then what other people are out there who might surprise me in a good way? I've been *un*pleasantly surprised enough.

chapter 15

MONDAY IS FILLED WITH RINGING
telephones and lame excuses on voice mails that I delete before
they're finished. I throw myself into making a new skirt, fan-
cier and more complex than my others due to all of the buttons
I'm sewing onto it. I call it my Frog and Toad skirt, like in the
kid's book where Frog and Toad go searching for Toad's lost
button, but all they find are wrong buttons. In the end, Frog
gives Toad a sweater covered in all of the found buttons. Or
was it Toad gives Frog? Either way, that's what a real friend
would do.

I listen to a new audiobook, *Elsewhere* by Gabrielle Zevin,
about a girl named Liz who dies and lives her death in a place
called Elsewhere, aging backwards until she turns into a baby
again and travels back to Earth. The reader has an elfish voice,
which I first thought might annoy me, but now it seems perfect. Liz is all pissed because she'll never get to be able to do
all of the normal teenage stuff, like driving and prom, and she
misses her friends. I slap myself away from the thought that
maybe I'd be better off in a place like Elsewhere. Not dead, of
course, but if I aged backwards, then all of this horrid friend

crap would be a thing of the past. And I'd know what a traitor Bizza is ahead of time, so I could find much better friends to spend the rest of my impending childhood with. A skirt and an audiobook, and I still can't get Bizza off my brain.

Barrett comes into my bedroom with the phone held out in front of him. "Phone. It's Bizza. Again!" he yells the last word into the receiver.

I announce in a voice loud enough for anyone on the other end to hear, "I am not taking any calls today or EVER from said caller."

Then Barrett puts the phone back to his ear and says in an overly soothing, breathy voice, "I'm sorry, Jessica is unavailable right now. May I take a message? Hey! She hung up."

He sits down on my bed and watches me sew buttons. "So what did you think of Chloe?"

"Chloe Romano?" I tease him. He doesn't even bother to respond. "She seemed really cool. Smart. Not at all what I expected."

"I know," he says dreamily, and falls back onto the bed. "I'm going to marry her."

"What?!" I stop sewing. "When?"

"Not soon or anything. After college, of course. She's amazing. Perfect. She's my Sloan Peterson." Barrett has been obsessed with Ferris Bueller's girlfriend, Sloan Peterson, since he saw *Ferris Bueller's Day Off* in sixth grade. He used to talk about marrying *her*, saying how excellent it would be that her married name would be "Sloan Sloan." Chloe Romano must be pretty special. "I'm thinking of asking her to homecoming."

"Yeah, I think homecoming would be a better first step than marriage. But since when do you go to school dances? I thought you hated that crap." I sew on a strawberry-shaped button I found in our kitchen junk drawer and wonder where the other strawberries are.

"Technically I still do. But Chloe's been hinting at it. Like, 'As last year's homecoming princess, I'd hate to go without a date.'" He says this in a la-ti-da girl voice.

"Doesn't that go against all of her feminist principles? Beauty contests and ho-ing it up in a fancy dress?"

"She explained it to me like it's some social experiment. She figures it'll make a great thesis when she's in college."

I feel a pang in my chest with the reminder of Barrett's eminent departure for college. How will I make it through two more years of high school without him here to drive me around and make fun of my crappy friends?

"You know," I say, "with Chloe Romano as your homecoming date, you could be homecoming king." Barrett lets out a scream of terror.

I work on the Frog and Toad skirt until my mom calls me down to dinner. We usually have pizza bread on Sunday nights to soften the blow of going back to school/work, but since we didn't have school today, pizza bread has been shifted to Monday's schedule.

"TGFPB," my dad declares, his dorky way of saying "Thank God for Pizza Bread." He says this every week. I think pizza bread may be his religion.

After dinner I finish up the last of my homework. As I wash my face, I'm surprised at how unbad I feel about the whole Bizza/Van thing. Maybe it's just the Zenlike state of precalc. I mean, of course I feel sucky, but not so much because of the betrayal as because I might have to run into them and that's going to just be totally uncomfortable. In fact, I can truly say that I would be absolutely fine if neither of them were in my life ever again. Char, too. Even though she didn't technically do anything to me, she didn't *do anything*. Tell me or tell Bizza before this turned into what it did. That's almost as bad.

I fall asleep thanking god that my parents made me smart so I don't have to be in classes with my idiot ex-friends. Tomorrow, my quest for new friends begins. I hope they keep their shirts on.

chapter 16

I PUT ON ONE OF MY FAVORITE skirts, made from Wonder Woman fabric. I hope her Amazonian strength helps me through the day. Just to be a little different, I part my hair on the left side instead of the right. It doesn't fall quite the same way and adds a slight pouf to the front. Nothing radical, but kind of glamorous, I decide.

On our way out, Barrett stops to look at me for a second. "There's something different about you," he says.

I want to tell him that today I leave the house a free woman, open to the possibilities of new friendships and happier times. Instead, I just say, "I parted my hair on a different side."

Barrett grunts like he's thinking about something else. "I don't want you talking to Van," he says, "even if he talks to you. I could beat his ass after what he did to Bizza." I feel a twinge of *ugh* that Barrett is acting protective of Bizza and not me. "He has no respect for girls at all." I realize he's spouting Chloe speak and don't feel as bad. Plus, I really wouldn't mind Van having his ass beat. When I was younger, I used to take tae kwon do. It was so major kicking boys' butts when we sparred. I quit when I got boobs and felt too embarrassed to do jumping jacks (pathetic, I know), but I always wished that I had kept it up. Sometimes I envision myself in situations, usually after someone has obnoxiously knocked my books out of my arms or stepped on a brand-new pair of shoes, where I execute a brilliant roundhouse kick and totally take some pudhole down. I catch myself in that moment, clenching my fists in the middle of a crowded hallway, and wonder if anyone knows I'm thinking violent thoughts. In a way, I'm a little jealous of Barrett. Not that I want to get into an actual fight, but it must be empowering to believe that you can kick someone's ass. And Barrett can definitely kick Van's. I doubt he will, though. Not when he's trying to get into college and someday marry Greenville High's top candidate for homecoming queen. Plus, he's above that.

My shoulders are back, and my head is up as I walk through the halls to my locker. I refuse to worry about what may happen if I see Bizza. Confrontation, even when I'm completely in the right, isn't my idea of a good time. Especially with Bizza, who I know will try to turn this into something *I* did to make her do what *she* did. And she probably doesn't even care. She did call about a thousand times yesterday, but maybe that was to recap every Krispy Kreme moment of her Van Blow Job Extravaganza. For a moment, I slump in disgust, but then I regain my superstrong Wonder Woman posture and head to first period.

Polly is beaming a "guess what I did this weekend" look

my way. She is wearing an uncharacteristically tight, low-cut shirt that shows off her surprisingly bouncy cleavage. The pathetic side of my brain thinks, *If I had boobs like that, maybe I would have been with Van instead of* . . . But before I can finish that thought, the empowered side of my brain smacks the pathetic side and says, *Van is an asshole. Did you really want to be doing what Bizza did with him? And besides, your boobs are great!*

After English, and much wiser in the sexual ways of the band geeks, I make sure to take the direct, not the avoid-Bizza-at-all-costs, route to gym. I'm having a particularly vivid and violent fantasy where I throw Bizza through one of the courtyard windows and scream, "How's your haircut now, bitch?" when I'm snapped away by the hilarious sight of Dottie Bell and her nerd herd dressed in full medieval garb. I walk up to her. "Hey, Dottie. What's with the fancy?"

"Jessie! You noticed. No one else has said anything. To our faces, that is." The crew laughs. There are six people, one of which I recognize as Dottie's boyfriend, Doug, and another as Kent Holt, this kooky guy from my science lab. He's always getting our science teacher, Mr. Roland, to freak out by pretending he spilled acid on his hand. "We're preparing for Fudwhalla," Dottie continues. I look at her blankly. "It's this insane, live role-playing weekend in Wisconsin that's in a few weeks. I'm going to be a baroness." As she says this, her posse bows. I think of how opposite her royalty would be to

Chloe Romano's homecoming queen. "We want to make sure our costumes are comfortable enough to wear all weekend, so we're taking them for a test run."

"What's the verdict so far?" I'm genuinely intrigued. Amusing clothes are my passion, after all. Dottie sticks her hands down the front of her dress and pulls out bunches of crumpled toilet paper.

"Not so great, I'm afraid. We borrowed these from Philip's cousin who worked at a Renaissance Fair over the summer. They don't fit very well."

"And they reek," notes one of the guys in the back.

"I wondered what that was." I pretend to fan away some stink. "Not really," I say when it looks like they're taking me seriously (complete with numerous armpit sniffs).

"I was planning to talk about your sewing gift during study hall. Maybe proposition you for some help?" Dottie looks at me, hopeful.

My cheeks burn a tad. My *gift?* I have a gift? My moment of glory is stolen by the bell. "Gotta go!" I tell Dottie and her followers. "If I'm the last person changed, Ms. Honalee makes me do laps."

"We'll talk later." Dottie leads her troops away. As I pass, I make eye contact with one of the guys I don't know. He has unruly, curly brown hair and electric blue eyes that seem to be smiling at me. I hesitantly smile back before I turn away and run to the locker room.

• • •

At lunchtime I make some effort in my quest for new friends. Every day, Polly sits at a table filled with her fellow marching bandmates, many of whom I know from various smart-kid classes. I approach the table tentatively, a friendly smile on my face, and say, "Mind if I join you?" The band geeks look at one another questioningly, until Polly says, "Of course, Jessie! Scooch down, Chip." Chip Eddelson is a gangly, red-headed, big-gummed tuba player, and I hope he doesn't know it's me who threw tennis balls into the marching band practice area last year just to see if I could land one in his tuba (I could). At six foot four and approximately 110 pounds, I don't know how he manages to even hold up a tuba. I sit next to Polly, and lunch conversation flows with a mix of band and dating chatter. Polly explains, "We're together for so many hours and so many bus rides that practically everyone in the band has dated each other at some point."

"We're very incestuous." Chip arches his eyebrows at me, and I look down, desperately hoping he's not trying to bring me into his tubalicious lair. "I heard from someone that you play the drums, Jessie. You should try out." More like he's trying to recruit me.

"Well, um, with my homework and my sewing, you know, I just don't have time for much extracurricular stuff." I weakly try to talk my way out of it. I haven't exactly had the best luck with bands.

"But the extracurricular stuff is the best part," Chip sleazes. Definitely *not* tubalicious.

"Chip, don't scare Jessie away with your band wet dreams." Saved by Polly. "And anyway, Jessie, you know what they say: the bigger the instrument, the smaller the . . ."

"Hey! My mom chose the tuba for me! I wanted to play the flute. Or the piccolo!" Chip unsuccessfully backpedals.

"How manly of you," Polly retorts. And conversation (thank god) moves away from my involvement in the band to other, less me-centered topics.

At the end of lunch, I'm happy to have found a new group of people to eat with. Without my full commitment to the band, I can't see us hanging out outside school situations, but I'm at least trying to open up my possibilities.

I'm on a new-friend high when I run into Bizza in the hall. She looks less annoying than usual, without black eye makeup and her "trademark" kilt. Actually, she looks pretty crappy (and I'm not just saying that because she sucks). If it's possible, her buzz even looks like she didn't fix it today.

She catches my eye before I'm able to avoid her, and she walks up to me, slouched. "Hey, Jess," she says with a desperate smile.

"Hey," I respond coolly.

"I tried calling you yesterday."

"Yeah, I know," I jump in quickly, trying to move this uncomfortable conversation along.

"I hope you're not still upset. It was no big deal. . . ." She's not as ballsy as she normally is, but it's still so Bizza to not apologize, but to make it seem like I'm the one making something out of nothing. I don't speak.

"What are you doing after school?" she asks. An interesting turn: Bizza *asking*, not *telling* me what I'm doing. Still, I don't feel like talking to her.

"I have to get to study hall." I walk off, leaving her to end the conversation by herself.

I'm halfway angry, half pumped with pride when I sit down next to Dottie. She's changed out of her medieval garb, which I'm kind of happy about. I like talking to her during study hall, but that outfit was pretty extreme. Plus, I don't see how she'd fit into the desk.

She starts talking at me the second I sit down. "Here's the deal, Jessie: Fudwhalla is in three weeks, and we desperately need new costumes. We'll pay for all of the materials, and Doug said he could make you something to make up for your time. He's wicked with a lathe."

"A what?"

"Woodworking."

"Oh. I don't know, I really only sew skirts. I mean, besides a couple of aprons and some curtains. I don't know if I can make whole costumes."

"You totally could!" Dottie is uncharacteristically animated and speaking too loudly. The study hall teacher's subtle "ahem" makes her take it down to a yelling whisper. "Can you follow a pattern?"

"Well, yeah."

"That's all we need! You're a fantastic seamstress, Jessie. Just look at your hem!"

No one has ever called me a seamstress before. It feels so official, like I don't just sew for fun; I sew because I'm good at it. I look at my hem and follow it around with my thumb, the way Van had once done so seductively. My skirts aren't just cute like everybody has so generically told me; they're well made. My stitches are even, my hem straight, my zippers undetectable. But whole costumes? "I'll think about it," I tell Dottie.

"Maybe if you come to D&D on Friday, we can convince you." I know she sees the apprehensive look on my face. "It's not as dorky as it sounds, Jessie. Really. I think you'll like it. Everyone is really nice. . . ." I drift off as she continues her sales pitch and think about that guy with the curly hair. He did smile at me. I wonder if he'll be there. Without tights, of course. "And there's tons of food." She's still going.

"Okay," I say with just the slightest hesitation. It can't hurt. I don't think.

"Wow. Excellent. I'll give you all the details on where and when later on. Cool." She looks genuinely happy, and I feel good that I have definite plans for Friday night. That jerky voice in my head pipes up before I can stop it and says, *You're going to play Dungeons and Dragons with a bunch of nerds on a*

Friday night. Are those really the kind of new friends you want to be making?

I glance over at Dottie, who flashes me the thumbs-up. Am I ready for this to be my new social life? I remember Barrett's reaction when I first told him I was talking to Dottie in study hall. I believe he used seventeen variations on the word *dork*. But it's not exactly like he's hanging out with the coolest people anymore. I mean, Chloe's cool in the popular, homecoming, hottest-girl-in-school kind of way, but not in the freakster, hair-dyed, giant-shoes kind of way that Barrett taught me to covet. Maybe he will be better at accepting my Friday night plans than I expect. Maybe even better than me.

chapter 17

I STUDIED AFTER SCHOOL IN THE
library until they kicked me out, hoping it was long enough to
avoid the punk nasties. Barrett started his new job at the movie
theater right after school today, training—with benefits, I'm
sure—with Chloe Romano.

My walk home is long, but my backpack is lighter than
normal after I ditch my finished homework in my locker. I
listen to *Elsewhere* on my iPod as I walk with my hands on the
front of my thighs, trying to stop the wind from grabbing
onto my skirt in a Marilyn Monroe-esque gust. The narrator
has me completely immersed in this life-after-death world,
where some people can speak directly to animals. We've never
had the joy of a real pet, due to Barrett's severe allergies. The
only pet we ever had was a Beta fish named Bernard. He was
purple, red, and pink, and looked so fancy to me as a kid in his
perfectly round bowl. I don't know what my parents were
thinking when they made it my responsibility to clean his
bowl. Two weeks after his arrival, Bernard floated belly up in
his scum-covered water. But he was so young! So beautiful! I
couldn't get rid of him just yet. So he stayed in the bowl. For

weeks. Once the water evaporated, Bernard decayed quickly on the scum-colored rocks at the bottom of the bowl. I kept him just outside my window ledge so no one would notice. My dad finally discovered him when he was pruning the trees in our front yard. I wonder what Bernard would have said to me if he could communicate. I'd like to think that as he faded away, his forgiving fish soul would tell me, "It's okay, Jessie. You are just a young girl. My life was a short but happy one. Godspeed. I see a bright light ahead. . . ." But what he probably would have said was, "Why didn't you clean my bowl, bitch?"

When I arrive home, a little sweaty but stress-free, I find Doc Mom in the kitchen rolling matzo balls between her palms and dropping them into a giant pot on the stove. The air smells chickeny.

"It's a tad warm out for soup, isn't it? You usually don't get matzo ball cravings until at least after Halloween."

"My throat's a little sore. I think I'm getting a cold. Damn kids. If they're sick, their parents should keep them home."

Mom definitely sounds like she's getting something; she's not usually this cranky about her students. "Do you want some help?" I ask. I love rolling mushy food between my hands. Cookie dough is my number one favorite (particularly when it has chocolate chips, which act like little hand-massagers), but the sticky goo of the matzo balls is pretty nice, too.

"If you wouldn't mind rolling the rest of the balls and dropping them in the broth, I'll make some tea." Mom unties her flowery, frilly apron and passes it to me. I'm careful not to catch my hair as I tie the strings behind my neck. Patting a small lump of matzo meal out of the bowl, I roll it into a perfect circle before I toss it into the pot. A tiny splash of chicken broth sprinkles onto the stove.

"Careful, honey, try to not make it splash." Mom sits down at the kitchen table and waits for the tea to whistle. "How was your day?" she asks, and I wonder how many times that gets asked around the world every day.

"Fine," I answer, as expected.

"We didn't get to talk about Van's party on Sunday. Barrett told me he quit the band, which I can't say I'm sorry about. I'll finally get to fall asleep at a decent hour on a Friday night." Mom laughs uncomfortably, and I know she's going to bring up something I don't want to talk about. "I couldn't exactly ignore all of those unanswered phone calls yesterday. Was it Bizza?"

My mom has known Bizza since pre-every phase she's been through, and she's definitely seen both her good and bad sides. Good: How Bizza used to travel with our family every summer to Bane's Lake and would humor my mom with a mind-numbing game of Boggle while I attacked the water slides. Bad: How Bizza lied to my mom about "borrowing" my mom's only pair of Manolo Blahniks (which she won in a bidding war on eBay) and somehow managed to break off one of the heels before randomly tossing them back in my mom's closet (wouldn't you at least try to make it look like nobody moved them?). My mom accused me forever, and I finally gave in and told her I did it just so she wouldn't be mad at Bizza. What sucked about the whole thing was that my mom knew Bizza did it (they *always* know), so I was doubly bad in her eyes for a) lying and b) covering for a friend who would do something like that to me. Mom seemed to be forgiving because Bizza has continued to be invited on family trips, as well as holidays and other "family only" events. Part of me wishes my mom would have been so disgusted by Bizza's behavior that she would have forbidden me from seeing her ever again. Preferably before the onset of puberty, so I could have avoided any and all Bizza skank adventures.

"Bizza is no longer my friend," I declare, and I toss a matzo ball a little too violently into the pot. A giant plop of chicken soup lands on my arm. "Ow!" I yell, wiping it away.

"Careful," Mom says momily. "How long will *this* fight last?" She's seen countless fights between me and Bizza, lasting from one hour to three weeks. The worst (so far) came after Bizza stayed with my family for two weeks in eighth grade while her parents took an anniversary cruise through "The Islands." I don't remember what the fight was about, but it might have just been exposure overload. It ended in English class when Mr. Rowley automatically paired us up for a Shakespearian parody project, and Bizza kissed my ass until we made up and I agreed to write the whole project myself (she wanted an A).

"Forever," I answer.

"Wow. That long? What's she done now?"

I love how my mom automatically sides with me. Partially it's because she knows Bizza all too well, and partially because, well, she's my mom. "More like *who'd* she do." I chuckle at my wordplay until I see the panicked look on my mom's face. "Just kidding, Mom." Moms don't have to know everything. "Remember how I kind of had a crush on Van?" Mom sighs and nods. "Well, Bizza kind of, you know, hooked up with him." I sag at the reminder of betrayal. What a crappy thing for a friend to do.

"Oh, honey." Mom stands up and puts her arms around me. "I'm sorry. But don't worry, there are plenty of Vans on the road."

"Mom!" I can feel her smiling into my shoulder. Then she starts laughing.

"I couldn't resist."

"How long have you been saving that one?" I laugh with her, happy to lighten the mood and avoid more matzo ball burns.

"Too long," Mom answers. The teakettle whistles, and Mom pours herself a cup of chamomile tea (the Peter Rabbit cure-all). "Oh, Bizza," Mom says to the air. "Why couldn't you be a better friend to my baby?"

"Your baby?"

"You and Barrett are my babies, and you're both growing up so fast. Barrett will go off to college next year, then you'll be gone in two years. Where does the time go?"

Ah, the Where Does the Time Go speech. Mom brings

this one out whenever she's feeling sentimental, like last summer when Barrett visited colleges. We always have to pat her on the back and assure her that we'll always love her and take care of her and when it's time, be sure to put her in a clean but not too expensive rest home that doesn't force her to eat tapioca.

"Jessie, I just want you to know that there are a lot of really great people out there. You may not meet them in high school, but you'll find them. And hopefully they won't be as concerned with how cool they are more than how much they like to be around you. Because you really are a wonderful person, Jessica." Mom goes on for a while about how special I am and how lucky she is to have a daughter like me. The usual. I do think a little about one thing she says: "Hopefully they won't be concerned with how cool they are." I don't think I'm going to have to worry about that on Friday night with Dottie and the dweebs.

I interrupt Mom's motivational speech (not out of rudeness, of course, but to give her tired throat a break. Yeah.) to ask her, "Mom, if I decide I need to sew some elaborate costumes, would you be able to help me?"

"That's a rather random question, but I'd be happy to help you. As long as it's not a stay-up-all-night last-minute project. I swore I'd never let you do that to me again." Mom refers to too many Halloweens past where I decided the night before trick-or-treating that being a princess/ballerina/Dora the

Explorer wasn't cool enough, and I'd much rather be a ghost/ firefighter/ninja or whatever else Barrett was that year.

"No last-minute work. I promise. If I even do it." I don't know why, but I can't get myself to tell my mom about Dungeons and Dragons on Friday. I'm afraid she might laugh or tell me that only weirdos play D&D and try to talk me out of it.

I finish the last of the matzo balls and head to the sink to wash the goo off my hands. Mom slurps her tea and waves me out of the kitchen so she can finish up dinner. Before I head to my room to listen to my audiobook, I pick up several volumes from the World Book Encyclopedia in our living room. The set was my mom's from when she was a teenager, and we took it from my grandma's house after she moved into an assisted-living home last year. The set is white leather (or is it faux?) with gold writing on the covers. The date on the side glows "1975," which is why the encyclopedias are practically covered with dust. With lots of the information completely outdated (or just too groovy), Barrett and I never touch the books. I thought I might find some good pictures, though, in the sections on medieval England, knights, costumes, and royalty for the costumes I might sew. I laugh as I flip through the pages and remember the TP stuffing in Dottie's chest. Then the curly-haired guy pops into my head for an instant, before I shake him away and bring the heavy volumes to my room. I catch myself unintentionally smiling in my mirror.

chapter 18

MY ALARM ANNOYINGLY BUSTS ME awake from a glorious dream. The obnoxious rambling of the morning DJs wipe away any clear picture of who or what it was about, but I have that naughty feeling where I'm thankful I'm not a guy or I'd be changing the sheets right now. I roll around to stretch a little, wishing it was Sunday so I could go back to sleep and have my unruly subconscious continue where it left off. But if I don't hit the bathroom now, Barrett will hog it with his midweek head shaving, and I'll have to brush my teeth with his tiny hairs in the sink (the combo of spitty toothpaste and hair grosses me out).

Today is Wednesday, hump day, and I have managed just the one run-in with Bizza yesterday. She looked horrid, so maybe Van dumped her, if they were ever actually going out. Why do I care?

Before first period, I stuff books into my locker and sense someone hovering behind me. Part of me hopes it's one of my new nerdish friends, while the tiniest part of me hopes it's Van (I think my brain has some chemical addiction to him because my heart has very little interest). It ends up being Char, who I haven't seen or spoken to since the party. Her loyalty is obviously with Queen Bizza, but I feel a squeeze of happiness to see her. She's not smiling, though.

"Hey, Jess, how ya been?" she asks. Is she referring to how I've been since The Incident, or how I've been doing at school, or with my skirts, or with my complete and total transfer of social groups?

"Pretty good," I try to answer in as neutral a way as possible, not overly stoked to be talking to her, not flaming angry, just *chill*.

"Have you seen Bizza?"

Why is that always Char's question of choice? I flash back to when she asked me that on the first day of school and I saw Bizza's new head. "Why? What does her hair look like now? Is she totally bald? A faux hawk? Ooh—maybe extensions?"

Char interrupts my snarkiness. "No, I mean, I haven't seen her since yesterday at lunch. She and Van had this huge blowout in his car." I look disgusted. "I don't mean *that* kind of blowout. I mean like a fight. She was crying really hard when she got out of the car, and then she just disappeared for the rest of the day. I tried to ask Van what was the what, but he just asked me what I was doing later." She looks all annoyed, but my stomach churns at the thought. At least she didn't hook up with him, too.

"Haven't seen her," I tell her, and add coldness to my

voice to see if Char notices, but she just chews the inside of her mouth nervously. Feeling guilty, I add, "Did you try calling her at home?"

"Not today. Last night she didn't answer her cell or her home." Don't get me started on why Bizza needs a cell phone and a private home phone line. Probably to keep up with her prostitution business. Ouch. Did I just think that? "I'm gonna go and see if I can get in touch with her. See ya."

As I walk to first period, I'm kind of bunged that Char is so concerned with Bizza and doesn't seem too concerned about me. She once told me that it only *seems* like she sides with Bizza more when we fight, but really it's just because Bizza is such a drama sucker that if she doesn't make Bizza get over herself, we'd never make up. And Char hates when we fight. But how does that apply here? I think it's more like Char finally had to choose a side, and she's gone with the more socially active option. My Char analysis has me spacing out, and I accidentally crash into someone with a resulting shower of textbooks. "Dang! Sorry." I scramble to separate my books from my collider's, when I look up to see the curly-haired guy from Dottie's Rena-crew. My brain sparks, and I realize *he* was the guy I was dreaming about this morning that got me all hot and bothered. Flustered, I concentrate on the stacking of books.

"Hey, you're Jessie, right?" His voice is low and kind, and I wonder if that's how he sounded in my dream. It's not like I've ever really heard him talk before. What was he doing in my dream in the first place? "Right?" he asks again, and looks at me with intense, Flavor-Ice blue eyes.

"Uh, right." I just want to grab my books and go, but seeing as I dreamt about him, I should at least get his name. "And you are . . ." I hope it's not obnoxious that he knows my name but I don't know his.

"Henry." He rests his books on his crouched knee and extends a hand for me to shake. "Henry Hathaway." I grip his hand, and he gives me a friendly handshake, not too wussy but not all business-suit painful. A spray of curls falls over his eyes, and I'm almost grateful when the bell rings.

We both scramble to get our books and stand up, myself way too quickly. "Whoa." The blood rushes to my head, and I grab on to the closest thing to steady myself: Henry's chest. He balances my bobbling books on top of his stack while I compose myself (and notice the unexpected solidness under his baggy red T-shirt. Weird).

"Thanks." I regain my balance and my books.

"So I'll see you at D&D on Friday? It's at my house. Dottie can give you directions." If there was ever a way to excuse myself from a Friday night nerdfest, it's gone now. They all know I'm invited. And it's at Henry's house. The surprise subject of my I-wish-I-could-sleep-forever dream. Or maybe that's a reason I *should* excuse myself. What if he used some medieval magic to engrain himself in my subconscious?

I watch Henry walk away from me down the hall. His pants are a little too short, like he hasn't bought new ones since his most recent growth spurt, and he has on white leather gym shoes, the kind that I would only be caught dead in if I were on a far-off family vacation where I was guaranteed not to see anyone I know or anyone I would want to know. I must be in the Twilight Zone because I think maybe, possibly, somehow I might be crushing on a nerd.

chapter 19

I WAS AFRAID THAT DOTTIE WOULD
see. She has that freakish ability to know what I'm thinking
about, and if she figured out that I was thinking about one of
her crew, she might take it to mean more than it does. Which
is nothing, because I don't even have a choice in the matter;
my subconscious started this whatever-it-is. But according to
Freud, your subconscious is your *true*, hidden feelings. So
what does *that* mean?

Thankfully, Dottie is fully immersed in creating what she
calls "the most pwnage-inducing adventure you have ever
seen. Well, it's your first adventure, so it will be kick-ass no
matter what. Right, n00b?" She has taken to calling me "n00b,"
which I know is a dis, but Dottie claims is just a term of endearment for "role-playing fresh meat." Yes. Endearing.

I try to work on an English essay assignment, but I can't
seem to get my brain to stop drifting to Henry . . . Char . . .
Bizza. If this Van thing never happened, I'd be right there
with Char calling Bizza at lunch, stopping by after school with
crappy gossip magazines, helping her through whatever she's
going through. But I have to get it into my head that this

friendship is over. Friends don't treat friends the way Bizza treated me, and besides, I've got new sort-of-friend-type people who actually want to hang out with me, not use me to get through the punk cloud of smoke at Denny's.

I turn to precalc (maybe something more concrete will keep my mind from wandering), but I can't shake this guilty feeling I have about Bizza. Kicking myself all the way, I get a bathroom pass and head for the farthest stall in the most remote girls' bathroom. Cell phone use is against the rules during school hours, but I don't exactly feel like arguing with the hall monitor about why I need to call my friend from a pay phone in the middle of the day. Hopefully, no one will hear me. Bizza's number is still programmed as number 2 on my phone. I thought about deleting her, but that seemed so permanent, like once her number's gone I no longer have the ability to contact her if I really need to (ignoring the obvious fact that I've had her phone number memorized since first grade, and I couldn't forget it if someone dropped an anvil on my head).

I lean against the inside of the stall door. (I'd sit on the toilet lid, but for some reason our school bathrooms don't have lids. Maybe to prevent us from sitting on them and talking on the phone when we're supposed to be in class.) A cigarette butt floats in the toilet bowl, and I wonder how anyone managed to smoke in the bathroom without some suspicious authority figure smelling it. Maybe that's why the bathrooms always smell like an overload of generic celebrity perfume—to cover up the cigarette stink. My mind continues these (not so) enlightening observations until I get up the nerve to push 2. There are only ten minutes left in the period, and I refuse to be late to history, since Mr. Stein makes any latecomers wear a dunce cap. He claims it's been done this way throughout history. Maybe he wouldn't feel that way if he lived through the lice epidemic our school had in the third grade.

Bizza's phone rings three times, and then her mom picks up. "Hello?" she whispers, as though she knows I'm hiding in the school bathroom.

"Hi, Mrs. Brickman. It's Jessie. Is Bizza home today?" I whisper back.

"Jessie, so nice of you to call. I haven't seen you in ages. Are things going okay?" Mrs. Brickman continues to whisper. I'm a parental favorite, mainly because I rarely get into trouble, I'm polite, and I get good grades. Funny that my parents never got close with Bizza's or Char's parents; they mostly just waved from idling cars, waiting to pick us up.

"I'm fine, Mrs. Brickman. You?" I wish I didn't have to make nice with the clock ticking. Plus, every time I hear a noise from the hall, I'm sure it's the hall monitor coming to confiscate my phone. What if they think it's *my* cigarette in the toilet?

"Oh, okay. I took the day off work to take care of Bizza. She's not feeling well." I'm dying to make an allusion to the Van BJ at the party, but of course wuss out, when Mrs. Brickman says, "Sore throat. She's sleeping next to me on the couch, that's why I'm whispering. I told her if it doesn't get better by Friday I'm taking her to the doctor. And you know how she hates the doctor, so I'm sure she'll be good as new in no time."

Bizza has been afraid of the doctor ever since she had that prick test for allergies. Any time a needle comes near her, she goes screaming crazy.

"Do you want me to tell her you called?" Ig. Did I? I mean, I called to be nice, but leaving a message puts the ball back in her court. I don't want to jump with panicky avoidance every time my phone rings.

"That's okay. I'm sure I'll see her at school tomorrow." We hang up, just as the bell signaling the end of study hall rings. Instantly, girls with pointy shoes and giant purses fill the bathroom, and I escape before I'm covered in smoke and perfume.

chapter 20

I BEAT MY ALARM RADIO BY WAKING myself up this morning. I once read that you can remember your dreams better if you keep a journal next to your bed and write down everything you remember the second you wake up. You should do this at any point in the night you wake up, which I did, and which is why I am insanely tired. Now all I have next to me is a notebook filled with unreadable, crooked words. One page looks like it says "Turkey holiday," and I think I can make out "banana crepe" on another. Or is it "banana crap"? All I know is I don't see the word "Henry" anywhere in the notebook. Maybe I dreamed the whole dreaming-about-him thing in the first place. So at least that's taken care of for today. And my new phone strategy, just in case Bizza does get a message from her mom that I called, is to leave my cell off. That way my family has to screen calls on the regular phone, and she'll know my cell's off when it goes straight to voice mail. That's if she calls.

I knew I wouldn't be able to let it go.

• • •

Char greets me at my locker before first period. She's in some bizarre gold lamé catsuit, complete with severe cat-eye makeup and thick bangle bracelets shoved up past her elbows. I envy her nerve for a twinge, until she brings up Bizza. "So have you talked to Bizza yet? I called, but her mom said she couldn't come to the phone. Sore throat."

"That's as much as I know," I say, gathering my books. I wonder if Char will notice my new skirt, made with cute Elmo fabric I snagged at a baby sheet sale. Maybe she's blinded by her own golden glow because she doesn't say anything. Or maybe she doesn't even notice. Or maybe she does notice, but she doesn't want to say anything until I say something about her outfit. I'm not saying anything.

"I wonder what's wrong with her." Char looks overly concerned.

"It's a sore throat. Big deal. My mom's had one for a week. It's just something that's going around." Char's overanalysis of Bizza's everything annoys me, and I'm happy that she chose to bother me before instead of after school so I can make a clean getaway. The first bell rings, and I tell her, "See ya later."

"Yeah, okay." She pauses, with a stressed look on her face. "I hope I don't get Bizza's sore throat." I curse Char in my head that she *does* get it, but then I feel guilty and make her uncursed.

Polly smiles at me as I walk into English. We have an essay test about the significance graphic novels play in documenting history in the twenty-first century. I like this kind of test because it doesn't require as much studying as it does thinking, and Ms. Norton loves it when we get abstract and analytical (i.e., throw in a lot of big words and BS), so I know I'll do well. I smile back at Polly and notice how pretty she is—naturally red lips, bouncy hair, and she's so tall and thin. I look at her for a minute and try to take her out of context. Like, if she didn't go to this school and grow up with me and all of these people around us, and nobody knew she played the flute and was in the smart classes and dates a really goobery-looking guy—would she be popular? Would she want to be? A flash of Henry's bright eyes and curly hair pop into my head. What if Henry's pants weren't so short, his shoes not so white . . . How is it that someone becomes a dork? Do they choose to, just like Bizza and Char decided to turn punk? Are they born that way? What makes some people like punk music and Denny's and other people like costumes and Dungeons and Dragons? And where do I fit into all of this?

I try to clear all of the existential questions from my head and focus on my essay test. The BS flows nicely, and I leave class feeling pretty confident I scored an A. In fact, I did so well that I decide to make today an official A+ test day (yes, this is something I sometimes do), and I skip out on lunch with the band geeks in order to study for my precalc test in the library.

Oh. Henry's here. In the library. I don't want him to see me. Hide in the stacks, yeah, that old cliché hide-in-the-stacks routine so I can spy on the nerd who I may or may not have dreamt about. Because just sitting down near him instead of hiding from him would be weird, right?

My pathetic reasoning is interrupted by a scuffing sound coming from one row behind me. I peek through some dusty Einstein biographies to catch my brother and his homecoming bride making out. Yuck. I always try to avoid seeing my brother and his girlfriends in the act because I, nor does anyone else in the world, I hope, do not need to see Barrett's hand on some girl's butt. I don't care if she *is* the potential homecoming queen. Now I should really just bust out of here and sit down near Henry. I mean, I am going to his house tomorrow night, and—

"Jessie?" It's Barrett, who has extracted his hand from atop Chloe Romano's ass and is now standing behind me, watching me watch Henry. "What're you doing?"

I fumble a book off the shelf in front of me. "Oh, you know, just looking for something good to read." Barrett nods to the Enrico Fermi biography in my hands.

"Looks engrossing, dorklet."

"I'm not a dorklet." I stuff the book back onto the shelf. "And aren't you supposed to be in class? Not making out with Chloe Romano?"

"Are you spying on me?" No, I want to say, I'm spying on that nerd over there. "We both got bathroom passes. I'm going back to class now, Oh Hall Monitress. Enjoy your scientific discoveries." He pats me on the head in a big-brotherly, slightly condescending way. *Grrr.* I'm not a dorklet. I'm just going to sit with one.

I head over to Henry's table with the plan that it would be rude not to at least say hello, and if he offers me a seat then I'll take it, but only to study my precalculus. I try to be casual as I walk up, assuming he'll see me and the conversation will begin immediately. But he doesn't look up, and I recognize the white cords hanging down from his ears. I guess I could just sit down, or say something, or walk away really fast and pretend I never intended to sit with him in the first place. I decide on the last choice, but just as I move, Henry says, "Jessie?" Is it weird that I like the sound of his voice saying my name?

"Hey, Henry. I saw you sitting here, but I didn't want to bother you. Are you studying? What are you listening to? Do you have lunch now?" Why am I being rambly? It's not like I have to impress him with my coolness. Calm thyself.

"What?" He yanks out his earbuds, and I'm thankful he couldn't hear the game of twenty questions I was unintentionally playing with him. "Um, hey, how's it going?" Real smooth-like.

"Good. Just listening to Bob Dylan and studying for pre-calc. I pretend that the music helps me study, but I think it just gets songs stuck in my head and helps distract me from how stressed out I actually should be." He smiles, and I'm surprisingly mushed by the squintiness of his eyes.

"Who do you have for precalc?" I ask and sit down across from him.

"Ms. Jersen. Last period. So hard to focus on math at the end of the day."

"I heard she's hard, too." Conversation flows normally, and I figure he really can't see the Henry dream look on my face. Phew. I relax a little. "Do you want to study? I made flash cards of the formulas." I pull out some cards from my bag and notice that he's smiling even bigger at me now. "What?"

"Flash cards?" he asks me with an eyebrow raised.

"What?" I ask again. "What's wrong with flash cards?"

"Nothing, I guess. I just haven't used flash cards since I learned my multiplication tables. But you're the one with the straight As in math, so I won't question your methods any longer. Quiz me."

Wait a minute. Was I just made fun of by a nerd for being a math dork? And how did he know I was a math dork anyway?

We spend the rest of the period quizzing each other on formulas (where, by the way, I completely kick his ass). It's sort of fun, in a studying-for-a-precalc-test kind of way. When we get up to leave, I can't help but notice his floody jeans. Why do I care again?

"Thanks for your help. Maybe we can do this again next precalc test." He has amazing eye contact, and I'm a tad uncomfortable looking into his blue-raspberry-Slurpee eyes.

"Sure. But I may have to charge you," I joke. On the way to precalculus, I suddenly panic. I just helped a dork study for a math test. Wouldn't that make me an even bigger dork?

Mike Eastman passes back the tests without any comments about how I smell today. I put pencil to paper and ace the test.

chapter 21

DOTTIE VERSED ME IN THE BASICS
of Dungeons and Dragons all through study hall, but I barely
heard her. My nerd exchange incident really disturbed me. It's
like how I was thinking about Polly and how pretty she is, and
I was spying through the biography section, and then my
brother calls me a dorklet and I end up tutoring someone who
is supposed to outnerd me and where does that put me on the
social food chain? I have never been anywhere on it, technically. Like, if the school had to be divided into groups based
on social status, it would be so easy to say to most people,
"You go over there to jocks, and you go over to the dorks, and
you go over to the emo kids, and the punks, and the stoners."
And after all that sorting through the giant school strainer, I
would be left hanging out by myself still in the strainer because I wouldn't have anywhere to go. When I'm a senior, and
it's time to fill out our senior survey for most and best and biggest and hottest, I would be voted nothingest—except that I
wouldn't, because I'm so nothing that nobody would vote for
me. But what if I keep heading in the direction I'm heading
in—away from the punk god Barrett, away from the freshly

punk skag Bizza, and toward the nerd clan? Do I want to be voted biggest geek? Highest dork to the nth power? Tutor of nerds with ugly shoes?

I wish I could be like Bizza, ever the slutty, poseur skank that she is, because at least she can just decide to do something and go for it, screw what anyone else thinks. I mean, I could have been the one up in Van's bedroom with a shaved head, doing the deed, if I weren't such a nobody (and if I wasn't squeeged by the idea of a BJ, or if I wasn't afraid of what shape my head would turn out to be without hair. What if it was lumpy?). Well, I'm going to decide to do something. And that something is: nothing. I am not going to pursue the ho route that Bizza has taken, and I'm not going to play the drums and become a band geek, and I most certainly am not going to join Dottie and Henry (who *needs* to get out of my dreams) and a bunch of other dweebs to play Dungeons and Dragons, furthering my downward spiral into the position of First Official Dork. There. Decision made.

But what a lonely decision it is.

chapter 22

I MOPE MY WAY HOME, LISTENING to *Elsewhere*. Even in death, the character manages to find love, and it's so beautiful and so sad that I end up crying most of my walk home.

Dad is in the kitchen making corn bread to go with our chili dinner, and when he sees my face all puffy and red, he stops what he's doing and hugs me. "What's the matter, pumpkin?"

I sob, partly because of the ending of *Elsewhere*, but mostly because, as I put it so eloquently to my dad, "I don't want to be a nerd."

Dad chuckles a little but catches himself when he figures out I'm serious. "What makes you think you're a nerd? You don't look like a nerd to me."

I'm tempted to make some snotty comment about how he's not the best judge of nerd character, but I really do need someone to talk to about this. "I'm not a nerd yet, but there is definite potential for a nerdo-morphosis."

"Does this have something to do with your fight with

Bizza? You don't need a friend like her to be cool, you know."

"I don't need a friend like her, period," I say defensively. "But without Bizza, that means I have to find new friends, and the ones I'm finding aren't exactly what you or anybody else would call cool."

I expect my dad to be annoyed with my angsty bitching, but he surprises me with one word. "So?"

"So what?" I ask, confused.

"So, why do you need cool friends? It seems to me that your 'cool' friends"—he uses finger quotes, which I guess is where I learned it—"weren't very cool to begin with. And from what I've witnessed in this house over the years, Bizza was neither cool nor nice. Always telling you what to do, making you feel like you weren't good enough." Dad angrily stirs the corn bread batter and mutters incoherently on about Bizza. I am taken back by how pissed he sounds. I have never heard Dad say anything bad about my friends, and with the way he's talking, it sounds like he may have been holding back for a while.

"What's the deal, Dad?" I try to stop his mumblings before he stirs the corn bread into soup.

He takes a deep breath, dips his finger in the batter, tastes it with a satisfied nod, and pours it into a pan. "Jessie, you know I love you. And you know I would never say anything to try and influence your actions, because you're a smart kid, and you deserve to grow and make mistakes in your own way." He lifts his baseball hat off his head, smoothes his lack of hair, and puts the hat on again.

"You're boring me, Dad. Is there a point to this?"

"Bizza is a bitch. That's all I'm saying." He puts up his hands in surrender mode, then heads to the stove to stir the chili in its giant pot.

"Daaaaad," I elongate the word in a scolding way, but also with an underlying laugh. My dad is the Nicest Man on Earth. When my friends' parents can't be bothered to take us to the movies, he drives. When it's time to pick a vacation, he lets us choose the place. Even when he's talking about his worst, most turdly students, he does it in a fair and nice-ish way. Never has he sworn in front of me, and never has he given any reason for me to doubt the fact that he, too, was among Bizza's many admirers. "You think Bizza's a bitch?" He doesn't speak, but nods his head vigorously at the stove. I hope the grungy cap stays on his head. "Then why did you always invite her on our family trips? And with us out for dinner?"

"Because, honey, I knew you wanted me to."

I guess he was right, although there were more than a few times that life would have been better sans Bizza. "Then why didn't you ever say anything before?"

"Jessie, honey." Dad sits down at the kitchen table and pats the chair next to him. I sit. "As your father, as much as I wish I could, I can't pick your friends. Just like I can't pick your clothes or your music or your nose—"

"My nose?"

"Pick your nose. That was supposed to be a joke." I roll my eyes. "Do you see what I'm saying? You chose Bizza as your friend, and I had to accept it. Now, if you were planning on marrying her—"

"I'm not a lesbian, Dad."

"That's a whole other conversation. But I'm just warning you that I will tell you if I don't like whoever you decide to marry. In a hundred years or so, when you're ready to get married. We can discuss sex in another hundred and fifty years."

"No, Dad, we can't. But thanks for the weird talk."

"Anytime." I stand up to leave when Dad asks, "What makes you think your new friends are going to be nerds anyway?"

I sit back down to brace myself. Dad will be the first human being I tell, which makes everything one hundred percent official. "Ever heard of Dungeons and Dragons?"

"D&D!" Dad yells, and tosses his head back with a nostalgic laugh. "I haven't played since college. I used to love it. I didn't know you kids still played."

"*We* kids don't. Or at least haven't. I'm supposed to go over to this guy's house tomorrow night for my first adventure."

"Good times. Good times." Dad doesn't seem to notice

the confusion in my voice as his brain skips down memory lane. "Man, we used to play all night. That's one of the best things about going to college, by the way: no one to tell you to go to bed. We'd start at dinnertime, order a pizza, drink, order another pizza. . . ."

"Dad, spare me the debauchery." I already knew that my dad wasn't squeaky clean in college thanks to his marathon Just Say No speeches. *I had a friend, number one in his class, on his way to working for NASA. Hit the bud, and soon he was bottom of his class in Poultry Science. Even the chickens didn't want him. Stay away from drugs, or sleep with chickens!*

"Good point. You don't need drugs or alcohol to enjoy D&D. That's the beauty of it. You can become a completely different person in a different time and different place. . . . It's insanely fun. I'd still be playing if your mother hadn't made me quit."

I shudder at the thought of my dad and a bunch of other middle-aged men sitting around our kitchen table playing D&D on Friday nights. "Why'd Mom make you quit?"

I wait for the answer *Because only dorks play Dungeons and Dragons,* but instead he says, "Ah, took too much time away from our relationship. She never got it, and honestly, I think she was a little jealous."

"Of what?"

He does that hat lift-off thing again. "Yeah, well, I was

still playing after college when we both began teaching. She hated that I was spending my Friday nights with a bunch of people who weren't her. Plus, well, there was Simone." He says this name dreamily, to the point where I'm totally creeped. He notices my revulsion and clarifies, "Simone was the only female who played Dungeons and Dragons with us. Mom seemed to think I had some sort of crush on her."

"Did you?" I had to wonder with his far-out look.

"No, no, of course not. But I did always think it was cool: the lone girl at the D&D table, kicking troglodyte butt with the rest of us."

"You're scaring me a little, Dad," *because you sound like such a freak,* I want to add.

"You'll see. D&D is a blast. How long has it been since you lost yourself in play? Why should little kids get to have all the fun? Plus, you'll be one of the only females there, I assume?" I nod. "Prepare to be ogled, my dear. But not too much. One hundred and fifty years, remember?" Dad stands up, ruffles my hair, and goes back to chili cooking.

Our conversation has left me utterly confused. I would feel way too guilty at this point to ditch my first D&D adventure tomorrow night, but I fear that if I go, I open the doorway to nerd-dom, and there's no going back. I decide to make a pro and con list:

The Pros and Cons of Going to
Henry's Tomorrow Night for Dungeons and Dragons

Pros	Cons
It is Henry's house.	It is Henry's house, and why do I think that's a pro?
Seeing Henry in his natural habitat may curb my pervy dreams.	Seeing him for an extended period of time may burrow him into my subconscious permanently.
Dottie is really nice.	
D&D sounds fun—possible butt-kicking fantasy fulfillment.	If I become friends with Dottie, will people think I'm weird like Dottie?
It's better than staying home avoiding a call from Bizza.	If I think D&D is fun, am I automatically a dork?
What if Bizza doesn't call anyway?	
Why would I even want Bizza to call?	
Are these even pros and cons?	

I go to bed without any satisfaction from my useless pro and con list. Why do people make those, anyway?

I fall asleep willing myself to dream of anything but Henry. I decide not to do the dream journaling anymore, since I can't read it, anyway. I wake up at my alarm, realizing my will failed. In the dream, I'm wearing a fur outfit, but not like fur coats that rich old ladies wear. More like a caveman fur outfit. It's nice and warm, and for some reason I know I look pretty good. I'm sitting at a table in the cafeteria, and across from me, Van and Bizza are making out while holding Bosco Sticks in their hands. Bob Dylan is playing over the PA system, "Lay, Lady, Lay," which is a song I always liked as a kid because I thought he was saying "Lady Elaine," like that scary puppet from *Mr. Rogers'*. Anger grows inside me, and from out of nowhere I grab a sword. It feels light and comfortable in my hands, like a badminton racket. I feel someone's strong arms around my waist. I turn around into the naked chest of Henry, who's wearing only flip-flops and yellow flowered board shorts. He whispers in my ear, "Kick troglodyte butt," which in my dream I take to mean ram my sword through Bizza's and Van's cold hearts. I approach them silently and with a great roar, I swing my sword and— wake up panting and exhilarated. Not that I'd ever actually stab Bizza and Van with a sword (I mean, where do you even get a sword?), but the feeling of revenge in my dream was absolutely satisfying. I lie in bed for a couple of minutes to try and burn the memory of the dream into my brain. Revenge feels pretty sweet when you don't actually have to confront anyone.

139

chapter 23

I HAVE TO PEE, BUT BARRETT'S IN the bathroom shaving his head again. I thought he might decide to grow his hair into a Joe Normal preppie cut to blend more with his babelicious girlfriend, but he said he liked the way the buzz made him look a little mean. And so did Chloe Romano.

I pound on the door, and I know Barrett can hear me over the clippers but is choosing to ignore me. The aggression from my dream has made me a little pumped, and I smack the door open with the palm of my hand. *Whump.* "Damn" emanates from behind the door, and I giggle mischievously.

With the door cracked, I peek my nose into the bathroom. "Are you almost done, Buzzer? I have to pee." He clicks off the razor's safety guard and taps it into the sink. Taking his sweet time, he wraps the cord neatly around the clippers, stows the case under the sink, and admires his newly shorn 'do in the mirror. "I can pee just fine with you still in here, you know," I say, my legs crossed in desperation.

"No way." Barrett opens the door completely now, while I

bust past him to the toilet. "I can't stand the smell of pee first thing in the morning."

"Well, mine smells like roses," I call after him from my seat on the throne.

"Sure," he calls back, "just like your farts don't stink."

"They don't!" I protest.

We're almost late getting to school, due to my extra-long shower where I spend way too long overanalyzing my dream. Thankfully, my tardiness allows me to blow past Char when I see her in the hall. "Jessie—I need to talk to you!" she yells, but I just turn around and give a fake friendly wave as I speed away to first period.

Ms. Norton tells the class that if we leave her alone and actually do silent reading like we're supposed to, she should have our essay tests graded by the end of the period. I pull *Angus, Thongs, and Full-Frontal Snogging* out of my bag, which I have read about a hundred times, but I keep in my bag just in case I need something to read (or make me laugh). In it is one of my favorite lines of all times: "What in the name of Sir Julie Andrews?"

I'm chuckling to myself when Polly slides into the seat next to me. She smiles as she puts her books on the floor, except for her favorite note-scribbling notebook and a purple sparkly gel pen.

She begins writing a note that I know is to me, so I put the gum wrapper I use as a bookmark in *Angus* and wait. I can't help but notice more about her today, particularly her legs. Great legs is a concept that I've never really gotten on women (I mean, I can totally see why lean, muscley soccer-player legs on a guy can be way hot), since it seems to be a lack of muscle and fat (or any shape at all) that makes a woman's legs great, at least according to *US Weekly*. But when I look at Polly's legs, I guess I can sort of understand. And still, there she is: band geek.

What r u up 2 this weekend? She punctuates the message with a drawing of a face with questiony eyebrows. I know she's probably dying to tell me what *she's* doing this weekend, but I appreciate that she's polite enough to ask me first.

You'll never guess, I write, without any texty shorthand. I reserve that only for use with technological things. Sometimes it actually takes me more time to figure out what letters and numbers stand for than just writing the actual words.

Oooh—sounds kinky.

Doubtful. Why don't you tell me what you're doing this weekend first—with as few kinky details as possible, thank you very much.

My parents r letting me stay @ Jakes 4 the weekend, since it's a 2 hour train ride away. Can't wait! She draws little hearts around the whole note, and I feel happy for her.

I assume your weekend will be filled with high culture: plays, art exhibits, opera, I tease.

I'm not sure what he has planned. Lots of surprises, he said. But it's the 1st time I meet the parents. Yikes!

They'll love you, I'm sure. How can they not?

I know. ☹ Still scary! So I never guessed what you're doing. Big date?

No.

Skydiving?

No.

Nude beach?

As if. Give up?

Sure.

Playing Dungeons and Dragons with Dottie Bell and her friends.

I'm secretly hoping that Polly makes fun of me, to prove that Dottie and her friends are even lower on the social totem pole than the band geeks, but Polly just writes, *Fun! I tried once this summer, but it was way too complicated. My brother plays, and so does Jake. Who else is playing?*

Wow. That's it? Maybe she's just pretending she thinks it's okay.

I list the names of the few people I know, and Polly writes little comments next to them.

Dottie *She's been going out with Doug forever!*

Doug *is kinda cute!*

Kent Holt *hilarious!*

Philip Shen *I hear he reads a book a night. Way smart. Cute in a one-foot-shorter-than-me kind of way*

Henry Hathaway *He dated this girl from band camp last year. She said he's a really good kisser. Definitely cute.*

I stare at her comments in a state of shock. How is it that she manages to think everyone's cute that I think I'm not supposed to think are cute? Are everyone's brains programmed to think different types of people are attractive to ensure the survival of the species? I wonder what she'd think of Van. Yuck. I don't even want to think of Van. Sometimes I still do, though. At least I can ram him with a sword in my dreams.

Toward the end of the period, Ms. Norton starts calling out names to hand back our tests. Mine is an A, as predicted. Polly flashes her paper at me with a disappointed shrug. B−. I delicately show her my A with a guilty smile. She pretends to be mad at me by coming at my paper with her pen. I look around the room and catch glimpses of other people's grades: C−, B−, B+, with the majority in the B range. And I got an A. I take out the sliding nerd scale in my mind and push myself closer to the side that reads "Official Bona Fide Nerd." Now I just have to figure out if that's a bad thing.

chapter 24

WAITING IN THE LUNCH LINE, I KICK myself for the extra-long shower that prevented me from packing a lunch. The lunch ladies plop tomatoey, meaty lumps onto trays, and I smell what I believe to be sloppy joes. My stomach lurches at the thought of the pile of mushy meat atop a soggy bun. I consider having a minimalist Little Debbie vending machine lunch, when a hand taps my shoulder. I turn around to find myself looking up into Henry's curl-covered eyes. "I wanted to thank you for your help with precalc yesterday," he says. "I think I aced it. Although, you never know. We'll see this afternoon, right?" I nod and smile. He's so freakin' friendly, not like all of those aloof Denny's smokers, and not like the pervy, showy marching band guys. "I don't know if you have your heart set on a cafeteria lunch." I violently shake my head no. He laughs. "Do you want to go out?" He asks almost like he's asking a dog if it has to go out to pee. He catches himself and clears his throat. "To lunch, I mean. We could go to Burger King or Wendy's. Whichever you prefer."

Whichever I prefer. Nice. "Burger King, definitely." No more lunch Frosties for me, thank you very much.

We walk over to Burger King, talking (when we can hear each other over the traffic) mostly about teachers and classes on the way. Henry holds open the door for me, and I head to the end of the busy line.

"What'll it be, miss?" He takes out his wallet and flips through his money. "It's on me. For your help on the precalc test."

"No, don't worry about it. You don't have to pay." Part of me fears that if he pays, I owe him something. What I'd owe, I don't know, but I'd rather be debt-free for now.

"How about I'll pay this week, and you can pay next week. We can make this our weekly Friday celebration. If you want." It's very different being around Henry at lunch than being with Van. Van never really *asked* me about anything I wanted. It feels kind of chivalrous. A flash of Henry in surfer shorts pops into my head, and I tuck my hair behind my ears to push it away.

"Okay. Lunch out on Fridays. Unless there's a precalc test."

"But of course." Henry orders a cheeseburger and fries for me (which I told him I wanted) and two Whoppers, a large fry, and a vanilla shake for himself. I look at him quizzically. "Growth spurt," he explains. "It's freakish. I feel like a science experiment. Last year I thought I'd always be the short kid, and now this." He indicates his height. "Not that I'm complaining, but my mom can't keep up with me when she buys my clothes. She said she's giving up until I slow down a bit."

"Your mom buys your clothes?" I immediately worry that I sound bitchy, but it's a valid question, right?

He blushes as he collects our food and nods toward a booth. "I never really cared until they stopped fitting." He sits down and immediately tears into one of his Whoppers.

"But maybe if your mom didn't buy them, you could get the right size?" I try to suggest delicately. "So they're not so short?"

He laughs through his burger and wipes his mouth with a napkin. "Yeah. I guess I'm just being lazy. I'll think about it."

We eat and chat and laugh and smile, and I actually feel disappointed when he looks at his watch and says we have to start heading back. The traffic makes it nearly impossible to cross the street in time for the bell, so Henry yells over the noise, "Here—" and grabs my hand, weaving me in and out of the cars until we're safely on the other side. He promptly lets go, and I think maybe he just did it out of safety concern and not at all in any sort of romantic way. So what if I'm a little disappointed.

Before we part for our classes, Henry says, "So I'll see you tonight? Around seven?" And for a second I forget about Dungeons and Dragons and think we may actually have a date. "See if Dottie will help you make a character during study hall." Right. A character. For Dungeons and Dragons. Duh.

"What exactly does that mean?" I scrunch my nose in ignorance.

"To play D&D you have to be a character. So you pick a race and a class—like fighter or wizard or whatever—she'll help you. I'm guessing you'll be an elf wizard. Or maybe a rogue. But definitely an elf," he says in a knowing way.

"Why an elf?" I ask, almost insulted, although I have no idea why.

"Because girls like to be elves. Something to do with them being skinny and pretty." We're walking faster, so we're not late.

"Maybe I don't want to be an elf," I reply defensively. "Maybe I'll be a . . . troll." I picture the troll in the bathroom from *Harry Potter* and cringe.

"You can't be a troll." Henry's running down the hall now to his class, but turns around to yell back to me, "You're too cute!"

I blush and half smile, then catch myself and look around. Did anyone else in the hall see Henry Hathaway tell me I'm cute? Would it be so bad if they did?

chapter 25

AFTER I RECEIVE MY SECOND A of the day (A+, actually, on the precalc test), I run into Char in the hallway. Buzz kill.

"Hey, Jess, Bizza really needs you to call her. She has to go to the doctor today, and I can't go because of the twits. She wants you to go."

"What? Why? She said that?" I am totally thrown off by this. "Why do I have to call her? Why doesn't she call *me*?"

"She tried like a million times, but your phone was off. She really needs us, Jess." Char puts her hands around one of mine, like a grandma.

"Why doesn't her mom take her?" I refuse to let Bizza ruin my straight A of a day by using her annoyingly charming persuasive abilities to make me do something somebody else should be doing.

"She doesn't want her mom to know."

"But her mom already knows she's sick." I thought I was so out of this already.

"Actually, she thinks she's better now. That it was just a sore throat. She came back to school today so her mom wouldn't think that anything is wrong." Char lowers her voice, like whatever it is should not be common knowledge.

"What *is* wrong?" This is like one of those annoying sitcom conversations where no one is saying anything, yet they just keep talking.

"She thinks she has"—Char leans in for a dramatic whisper—"gonorrhea." I don't say anything, but look at Char with a look that demands her to go on. "I heard from this girl in my bio class who knows this girl from another school who dated Van for, like, three seconds, and she said that she had gonorrhea and she got it from Van."

Ickickickickickick. "Gross" is all I can get out.

"Yeah, no shit. She needs you to go with her to the free clinic after school. I'll see her at lunch. Can I tell her you'll go?" I sigh and look up at the ceiling, hoping to find an answer in the puckered tiles. Bizza may be a selfish bitch, but she was my friend and I know how afraid she is of doctors.

"Fine," I decide. "Tell her I'll meet her at her locker after school. But I'm leaving right when we're finished at the clinic. I have plans tonight."

"Thanks," Char says, and she kisses me on the forehead. I used to find her kisses sort of ethereal, like a kiss from such a beautiful person would transfer whatever she had to me. Today, it just feels condescending.

I don't have much time to process before I reach Dottie in study hall. She's expecting me, ready with an open hardcover book, a bunch of dice, and a pencil.

"Henry told me I was going to help you make your character. Good idea, so we can get right to the adventure at his house." Dottie is so serious and official, I press my lips together to hold in a laugh. I'm so glad she's here to help me forget about this new and infectious Bizza business. "The first thing you want to do is pick a race. Here are your choices." She holds open the book, which I learn is the *Player's Handbook*, to a page of beautifully drawn male and female humans and creatures, all scantily clad in armor.

"Henry assumed I would be an elf, so I should choose something else, right?"

"Totally. Why not be a dwarf, like me?"

I look at the picture of the dwarf, who is short, ugly, and asexual (but leaning toward extremely manly). Dottie looks at my face. "No on the dwarf, then? What about a gnome? Tiny and cute?" But the gnome is just as dudely as the dwarf, only smaller. I can't picture her wielding a sword in a furry bikini (à la my dream). I shake my head. "You could be a human." She says this like she just ate a brussel sprout. Even though the human in the picture does look kind of hot, I'm already a human. I shake my head. "Then how about a half-elf? You can always make up some story about how your parents were star-crossed, interracial lovers. . . ."

"Fine. Half-elf. Nice compromise." No lover (gross word) talk necessary.

Dottie takes me through the process of choosing my abilities, which consist of six traits that will determine how strong, smart, athletic, charming, etc, my character will be. I get to roll a bunch of dice and Dottie helps me distribute the numbers so my character has statistics that make her very strong, relatively flexible, and most definitely attractive. I know it's dorky that I want to pretend to be some hot, muscular chick, but as long as I'm going to be role-playing, I may as well feel like I look good doing it.

Next I have to choose my class, which is sort of like my job (if wizards and thieves were career choices). "Fighter," I say as I scroll down a list of choices.

"You might have more fun being a rogue or some kind of magic user—"

I interrupt Dottie. "I just want to fight. I don't want to have to think, or twitch my nose, or wave my wand or whatever. I want a big sword, and I want to swing it."

"How phallic of you. Fighter it is." She writes this down on my character sheet.

The rest of study hall is spent choosing my weapons, armor, and all of my skills. Dottie says the skills don't always help you in an adventure, but they give your character personality. I decide I'm going to be really good at gem appraising and oven-mitt knitting (which I said as kind of a joke, but Dottie said is totally legit if I want it to be). "Lastly," she says, "you need a name."

I assume people in the realm of Dungeons and Dragons do not have normal names like Amy or Beth. "Well, what's your name?"

"You must call me Dungeon Master." She puffs up and gives me a regal nod. "But when I'm a player, I am called Sofa."

"Like a couch?"

"Yeah. I thought it sounded mysterious."

"A couch sounded mysterious?"

"Shut up and pick a name."

I think for a moment before I decide. "Imalthia. Like in *The Last Unicorn*," one of my favorite books *and* movies.

"Oooh—good one." I do feel kind of proud.

The bell rings. "Well, Imalthia, prepare to kick ass. Or to get your ass kicked, depending on how I'm feeling tonight."

"Later, Sofa. I mean, *Dungeon Master*." I bow to Dottie. Then I remember what I have to do before my Dungeons and Dragons extravaganza begins. Bizza, a clinic, a doctor—if only it were Imalthia going on the gonorrhea adventure and not me.

chapter 26

I TAKE MY SWEET TIME DIALING THE combination into my locker, slowly placing books back in, slowly taking different ones out, checking, double-checking I have everything in my backpack. When my locker section clears out, I know I've procrastinated long enough. I just know Bizza will be at her locker, and I'll not only have to endure the torture of going to the doctor with her to find out if her fling with Van gave her gonorrhea but I'll have to look at her back-stabbing face or her gonorrhea-y mouth. Eeeww. Unless divine intervention actually works and Bizza magically turns into a loaf of bread or a Twix bar (I'm kind of hungry. . . .).

I half expect to find Bizza and Van making out against the lockers, just because that's kind of how things seem to work lately, but when I turn the corner into Bizza's locker section, I find a solo Bizza sitting on the hard tile floor, knees curled up to her face. She looks up when she hears my approaching feet, and I panic with an obligation to say something. What do you say when your oldest, ex-best friend betrays you by going down on the guy you had a crush on forever and now she needs you to go to the doctor with her because maybe she has *his* sexually transmitted disease? Does Hallmark make a card for that?

"Hey," I say, half solemnly, half pissed. She looks like crap—crappier than when she had her wisdom teeth taken out and her face swelled up like a Red Delicious apple. Her hair is a little fluffy, growing out from last week's buzz, and she has dark circles under her eyes. Instead of some elaborate punk ensemble, she's got on a pair of black Lucky sweatpants I remember her buying on sale (I bought the same pair in gray, even though I really wanted that black pair she's wearing now). Her sweatshirt is a completely unpunk Greenville High hoodie, which we also bought at the same time the summer before we started high school. Back when we thought it was cool to show school spirit.

Bizza speaks slowly. "Sorry to ask you to do this. I would've made Char come, but her brothers . . ." It's amazing how I can now analyze every word coming out of Bizza's mouth as selfish and bitchy. Why is her only apology that I have to come with her to the doctor? And how obnoxious that she thinks—and she's probably right—she can just *make* Char go with her. It's like the whole anti-drunk driving campaign: Friends don't let friends drive drunk, but tweak it to: Friends don't *make* friends do anything. God, what am I doing here?

Bizza acts the drama queen by crawling to her hands and knees on her way to standing up. The fighter in me wants to kick her while she's down, but that seems a tad violent. Plus, if she does have gonorrhea, then I guess I could say Van burned her already. Not that that makes up for anything. And where is Van anyway?

"Why didn't Van take you?" This is probably one of those questions I'm not supposed to ask, but I'm asking anyway.

She doesn't look at me, but slings her bag over her shoulder as she starts walking. "He won't talk to me. Not since . . . his party. I tried calling him. Left a note in his locker. He won't even look at me."

I am so glad I didn't hook up with Van. Even if it wasn't really my choice, I'm still glad. How can he treat her this way? Even though she completely sucks?

I assume Bizza wants some sort of sympathetic response, but just because I'm thinking it doesn't mean I have to say anything. All I do say is, "How are we getting to the clinic?"

"Bus. I can pay if you want." Oh really, Bizza, how freakin' generous of you! Seeing as how I wouldn't even be taking this bus if you didn't require my services. My blood is boiling, and I'm trying to remember why I'm doing this in the first place. We were once good friends, so that should count for something, I guess. If I were in this situation, I would want a friend with me, too. But probably not Bizza. And would I even get myself into this situation? I try to turn my brain on low thinking so I don't have to argue with myself the entire trip to the clinic. Just because we were once best friends, does that mean we always have to be?

It's strange taking the bus in the suburbs. I've only done it one other time in my life, when my mom's car was in the shop and my dad was out of town. I thought it was fun back then—putting the money into the slot, hanging on to the pole so I didn't fall when the bus driver overaccelerated, and pulling the cord to make the bus stop. It could have been just as fun today, except for the crappy company and our final destination.

I find a two-seater while Bizza drops coins into the money machine. The windows help me avoid any possible small talk with Bizza, and I watch the familiar strip malls and car dealerships swish by. About ten minutes pass when Bizza says, "We're the next stop." She looks down at directions printed off the computer. *Ding!* I pull the cord with an inner smile of delight. I wonder if that stops being fun if you take the bus every day. I don't think it could.

The clinic is packed, and I consider if Bizza even has an appointment. There's no way I'm waiting around for the next available doctor and missing my prep time for Dungeons and Dragons at Henry's house tonight. Bizza stands just inside the doors, looking around in a panic at the various lines, signs, and waiting areas. I follow her gaze to a sign that says WOMEN'S CLINIC. She doesn't bother to say anything, just assumes I'll follow her, and I'm about to say something pissy when I see the fear on her face.

We wait in a short line leading up to a window. I watch the circus of screaming babies and children in the vast waiting room. They should bring us here on a field trip as a form of birth control. How could anyone get pregnant after watching this chaotic freak show?

Bizza is handed a clipboard of forms to fill out, and we take a seat next to the divider that separates the women's clinic from the pediatric clinic. It doesn't stop the sounds of howling babies from the "room" next door. I don't know why Bizza needs me here—she isn't looking at me or talking to me or asking me important medical questions that I can't answer. I pull out my worn copy of *Angus, Thongs, and Full-Frontal Snogging* and start reading from the beginning. I'm actually on page sixty-six as of the last read-through, but who knows how long I'll be waiting here. I might as well make maximum use of the book. There are magazines spilling all over the place, but I hate to touch magazines in doctor's offices. Just in case.

I'm half reading, half watching Bizza as she hands her clipboard and fat doctor's office pen to the woman behind the counter. I can't hear what the woman says, but I hear Bizza loud and clear when she asks, "Can my friend come with me?" She looks back in my direction with pleading eyes. I can see the woman behind the glass form the word "no," along with some other words that I have no chance of lip-reading. Bizza stares at me like a doll whose eyes have been left in the extremely awake position. I feel for her and mouth, "You'll be okay." She mouths exaggeratedly, "What?" And I mouth again, "You'll be okay." And she shrugs her hands and shoulders up, like she still can't hear me. Before I can try again, a nurse appears beside her to take her back into the great medical unknown. The only supportive gesture I can think of that she can understand in such a short amount of time is to give her a thumbs-up. It's not exactly appropriate, but it seems to help a little as she produces the tiniest of thankful smiles. I hunker down in my plastic seat and prepare for the long wait, but Bizza appears ten minutes later, looking way relieved.

"They think I'm right about the gonorrhea, but it was so nothing. There were no needles. It was like a swab, sort of like a strep test. And the nurse said I'll probably only have to go on antibiotics, so no shot or anything. I have to wait to see a doctor still, but isn't that great?"

Shocked pause.

Deep breath.

Explosion.

"Great? What the frick is so great about this? You sucked a guy off—a guy *I* liked—who won't even talk to you anymore. He gave you a sexually transmitted disease because you were too friggin' 'in the moment' to use a condom, not to mention the fact that the *only* thing you got out of your bedroom visit with Van was gonorrhea! Was it good for you, Bizza? Was it worth trading your best friend for an asshole and some antibiotics?"

Stammering, Bizza tries to speak. "I only meant—"

"You only meant that this is great for *you*. 'Cause all that ever matters is what's great for you."

"I thought we were cool, Jess. I thought that's why you came with me."

"No. *We* are not cool. I came with you because part of me hated being mad at you. But you know what? I could give two and a half shits whether or not we're cool or if you think I'm cool, period. I'm done with this whole cool thing. You can keep on shaving your head and giving assholes blow jobs and then basking in the glow of antibiotic glee you seem to be enjoying, but I have better places to be. Maybe even dragons to slay." I dramatically stomp away, welcoming the glances of curious waiting room spectators.

I don't know if what I said will even sink a tiny bit into her inflated head, but I'm happy I had the chance to say it. Maybe deep down I knew that was the real reason I agreed to go with Bizza to the clinic. *I* needed to be cured of something, too.

chapter 27

I CALL BARRETT FROM MY CELL AFTER walking a good six blocks away from the clinic. I doubt that Bizza would follow me, partly because I think she's too self-absorbed to chase after anyone (except Van, and look at the nice parting gift she received), but mostly because she's still waiting to see a doctor. Luckily Barrett isn't working today, and he arrives fifteen minutes later with Chloe Romano riding shotgun.

When I called Barrett, all I told him was that I needed a ride and I would explain when he picked me up. Now I'm in his car, and I can't decide what to tell him. His questions are driving me nuts. "Are you okay? Did something happen? You're not prostituting yourself on street corners, are you?" He sounds almost serious, and I don't want him to worry (or keep asking me creepy questions).

"I was at the clinic," I start.

"The clinic?!" He freaks. "Were you having an abortion?"

I know it's not funny, but he is so out of control with panic that I bust out laughing. "God—no! Barrett, I wasn't there for me. . . ." Chloe strokes the back of Barrett's shaved head to calm him, and my heart jumps a little to see how much she really likes him.

"Shit—you scared me, Jess. You better not be having sex."

"You're such the role model of virginity, Barrett. And even if I was, it would be none of your business."

"Like hell it wouldn't."

He sounds like Dad. "Okay, I'll be sure to call you the next time I even get close."

"So why were you at the clinic, if you don't mind my nosiness?" Chloe interrupts, and I'm happy to get out of the brotherly sex talk.

"Well, let's just say an ex-friend of mine got a little present from an ex-friend of Barrett's." I don't know why I just don't tell them straight out. I guess I feel like it's not my story to tell.

"Bizza?" Barrett guesses. I nod at his eyes in the rearview mirror. "Van?" Barrett says Van's name through his teeth, and I kind of wish that we could pull over, or at least hit a stoplight so Barrett doesn't take this out on his driving. I nod again.

"So it's true," Chloe says. "I heard it from Jenna Grouse in the locker room, who said a friend of hers from Hillcrest used to go out with Van and thought that's where she got it, but he wouldn't talk to her, and—"

Barrett interrupts, "Got what? What the hell are you talking about?"

"Don't talk to me like that," Chloe snaps at Barrett. "Ask me nicely, and maybe I'll tell you." Chloe winks back at me, and I make a feeble attempt to wink back (I really have to practice my winks in a mirror). Barrett takes a deep breath, taps his fingers on the steering wheel, and comes up with, "Dearest Chloe, please, do tell, what the hell Van gave to this girl?"

"Why, Dear Barrett, I believe he gave her gonorrhea," she says in a noble voice. But that doesn't take the sting out of the air.

"And he gave it to Bizza," he demands an answer from me.

"I'm pretty sure. I didn't stay around long enough for the lab results." Barrett slams his hand on the horn, and both Chloe and I jump. A guy in the car in front of us gives us the finger out his window.

"Bare, chill out. You act like he did this to Jessie." She resumes her calming neck stroke.

"It could have been," he says quietly. "She liked him." Even if he is looking back at me in the rearview, I can't look at him. Maybe I would have been just as stupid as Bizza if I'd had the chance. Although hopefully the thought of Krispy Kremes would have stopped me.

"What we need to do now is make sure that Van doesn't do this to anyone else. You're going to have to talk to him, Barrett." Chloe sounds so grown-up when she says this, I don't see how Barrett can argue.

We're stopped at a stop sign, and Barrett leans his head forward into the steering wheel. "Shit," he says.

We sit at the stop sign for several minutes. Chloe continues with her neck stroking. They both seem pretty calm when Barrett starts to drive again. I, on the other hand, am building up some serious anger. Why is it that Van is allowed to do this to so many people and get away with it? Barrett may get him to go to the doctor or tell the million and a half girls he infected, but that's not enough for me. He may have hurt Bizza, but he hurt me, too. How many years of my life did I waste crushing on a total dick? What would Imalthia the fighter do?

chapter 28

I TRY MY BEST TO SHAKE THE
cruddy, confused feeling I have about Van and Bizza. It's 5:30,
and I only have a little over an hour to figure out how it is one
dresses for her very first Dungeons and Dragons adventure at
the house of my dream nerd. I know, I know, enough with the
nerd label already. It's just—if I take away the label, does that
make me officially one of them? If I hadn't been in such denial
over the past week, I could have found some fabric covered in
knights or dragons (or dungeons, I suppose, but I don't know
if that would translate well onto fabric). My closet is filled with
crazy skirts and plain tops, but nothing looks right for the occasion. I want to just look like the normal me—not too dressed
up, not trying too hard. Maybe just to show what a non-big
deal it is, I'll wear something totally casual. It's Friday night,
but it's just Friday night at someone's house. So it's not technically going-out where I have to wear going out clothes. Am I
overthinking this?

I opt for my Lucky sweatpants so I don't waste any of my
school skirts (yes, the same sweatpants I mentioned earlier
that Bizza and I bought), and one of my soft Lucky T-shirts,

red with a giant coy fish on it. It's obviously one of the least fancy outfits I could have chosen, but I do look good in red. And besides, who am I trying to impress? (Brain, don't answer Henry.)

I walk downstairs and realize I don't have a plan for getting to Henry's house. I just assumed that Mom or Dad would drive me, but they left a note on the kitchen table that they've gone out to dinner with some friends. That leaves Barrett. And that means I kind of have to tell him where I'm going.

Barrett has always been the one person in my life who taught me it's okay not to try and be like everyone else, but it always kind of felt like BS coming from someone so good-looking and smart, who just automatically knew how and where he fit in. I watch him from the kitchen doorway, sitting on the couch with Chloe Romano, one of the most popular girls in school, if not the free world, her legs draped over his lap. It was so easy for him to go from the King of the Punks to the Homecoming King (metaphorically, at this point, but it could happen) in a matter of weeks. But one thing he's never going to be is a geek. How will he feel about his kid sister turning into one?

I prepare for the worst, arm myself with defensiveness, and head over to the couch. Barrett and Chloe are nibbling on each other's various upper body parts, and I have to interrupt with an "ahem."

"Hey, Jess, I hope you don't mind if Chloe and I take over the TV. We rented some movies. You're welcome to watch, of course," which means I'm welcome to say that I'm happy spending the rest of the night in my bedroom trying to avoid seeing whatever Chloe and Barrett are doing to each other on the couch.

"Actually, I'm going out tonight. Well, going to someone's house. I didn't realize Mom and Dad weren't going to be home. Do you think you can give me a ride?" I hope that their interest in each other eclipses any interest they might have in what I'm doing tonight, but no such luck.

"Whose house? Not Bizza's, I hope." It's amazing how my family is so openly Bizza bashing these days.

"No. Just some guy from school. Name's Henry."

"A guy? Is this a date? Should I be giving you a lecture right now, young lady?" Barrett is overtly trying to impress Chloe with his protective-big-brother performance.

"Leave her alone, Barrett. Jessie's old enough to handle these things." I like that Chloe sticks up for me (and that I no longer think of her as Chloe *Romano*), but she's got the wrong idea.

"No, it's not like that. I'm going to his house, but there will be other people there."

"Is this a party? Should I give the alcohol lecture?" This is getting annoying.

"It's not a party!" I yell, frustrated.

"An orgy, then? Please say it's not an orgy."

"Barrett, the fact that you're even thinking about me going to an orgy tells me we're done talking about this. Can you please just drive me? The sooner we leave, the sooner you and Chloe can defile the couch."

"True." Barrett pauses, then lifts Chloe's legs off his and onto the floor. "Are you ready to go?"

"Yep."

"And that's what you're wearing?" Barrett eyes my sloppy ensemble.

"Yes, it is," I say indignantly.

He leans over to Chloe and says in a fake whisper, "Definitely not an orgy." Chloe shoves his shoulder, and we head off for the car.

Barrett blasts some late-eighties punk on the stereo, and I'm happy to see Chloe bobbing her head along next to him. It's good to see that he hasn't dropped everything from his old identity, and it's also nice how Chloe seems to embrace it. I tap Barrett's shoulder and yell into his ear every time he needs to turn, and eventually we end up in front of Henry's house just a little harder of hearing than we were before we left.

With the music this loud and Barrett and Chloe making googley eyes at each other, I'm almost free when who should come strolling up the driveway but Dottie Bell, hunched under her enormous backpack. The weight of the pack gives her a particularly slow and awkward walk, and I cringe that she had to look so nerdy when my brother and Chloe are watching. I bolt out of the car and yell, "I'll call you when I want to come home!" but I don't know if they hear it over the music. They for sure don't read my lips, because all eyes are on Dottie.

I don't want to look back for fear of seeing Barrett and Chloe peeing themselves with laughter, but my curiosity and optimism make me do it. It's so dark, though, that I'm not sure what it is I'm seeing. They're definitely not doubled over in hysterics, but I swear I can see incredulous, openmouthed stares. Or is that just a reflection? Before I can figure it out, the car starts to move.

Dottie turns at the sound of Barrett's car driving off, and she looks at me with an intrigued smile. "Jessie," she says in her relaxed way, "all right. Help me with this, would you?" Dottie carefully lowers her backpack to the ground and unzips to reveal two two-liters of pop, a stack of hardcover books, and a purple velvet pouch. I pick up the two-liters because I'm afraid that if I touch the books I'll be breaking some Dungeons and Dragons code about handling the Dungeon Master's things. Even though Dottie has on the same cutesy clothes she did at school today (green corduroy overalls, a T-shirt, and red cowboy boots), she has a look on her face that says not to mess with her. Truthfully, it's a little scary, and I try to prepare myself for what lies behind Henry's front door.

Amazingly enough, what lies behind Henry's front door is Henry, looking kind of adorable with his curls hanging over his Slurpee blue eyes, a plain black T-shirt, and . . . jeans that reach his shoes? He catches my gaze at his longer pants and says into my ear as Dottie and I walk in, "I went shopping after school *without* my mom. It was a little traumatic, I'd like you to know. Inseam measuring should be illegal."

"Was it worth it?" I ask.

Dottie leaves the foyer to greet her friends in the dining room with a resounding, "Cower before me, bitches! The DM has arrived!"

Henry looks at me with impenetrable eye contact and says, "You tell me." I catch my breath a little and break his gaze. His new jeans cover a good portion of his big white gym shoes, and I have an argument with my brain about how the way he looks shouldn't even matter, but he looks surprisingly good, sans the shoes, and I should stop being so judgmental, and . . .

"Let the pwnage begin!" Dottie yells from the other room. Henry grabs the two-liters from my arms and nods for me to go into the dining room ahead of him.

The dining room is crammed with a giant dark wood table and matching high-backed chairs covered in a regal, rich burgundy fabric stitched with golden thread. The walls are filled with bizarrely realistic, six-inch ceramic heads, all with frighteningly defined teeth. I scan the collection of fisherman, pirates, Beefeaters, and Middle Eastern stereotypes. Henry watches me and says, "They're called Bossons. My grandfather collected them and passed the collection on to my dad. He scours eBay every day to find the rare ones. You know, someday this collection will all be mine." He waggles his eyebrows at me, and I shudder exaggeratedly.

"You must be so proud," I say.

"Aren't you going to introduce the n00b?" someone yells from the table. I am the n00b, and I get introduced (and reintroduced) to the other four guys sitting around the table: Doug Emberly (Dottie's boyfriend), Kent Holt (the funny guy from my bio class), Philip Shen (lanky with smoky, metal-framed glasses), and Eddie Cotes (whose greasy brown hair looks like it got caught in a blender).

"Welcome, n00b, fear for your life," drips Eddie in a whiny voice, and I can't tell if he's joking until Dottie smacks him on his greasy head and says, "Don't scare her away yet, Ed."

"Yeah, Eddie," pipes in Philip. "Jessie's gonna help us make costumes for Fudwhalla. You better be nice to her, or she'll make you wear tights. Right, Jessie?"

Philip is so open and friendly, I don't want to say that I'm not sure yet if I can—or want to—make the costumes. Dottie sees my unsure look and asserts her Dungeon Master authority. "No more bullshit. We need to make some important decisions. What do you guys want on your pizzas?" The debate over the pizzas takes a half hour, and I try to be as easygoing as possible. (I never met people so passionate about pizza toppings.) Three pizzas are decided upon (half pineapple and ham, half pepperoni; half green pepper, half black olive, all onion; and half garlic and sausage, half plain cheese), and then another fifteen minutes are spent phoning it in, dividing up the money, and calculating the tip.

"What's the total?" I ask.

"$33.60."

"Okay," I figure out, "we each owe $5.60 for the pizza, and that should be another six or seven dollars added for the tip. Let's make it six, since that's just another extra dollar each. Everyone put in $6.60. Unless the delivery guy is really fast, then we can each round up to seven dollars for a nice tip."

You can hear the TV playing in the house next door, everyone is so quiet. They're all staring at me. "What?" I demand.

"Now you see why I'll never take a math test without Jessie again," Henry offers to the table. "I got an A, by the way." He tips an imaginary hat at me in thanks.

By the time eight o'clock rolls around, it's finally time to start playing Dungeons and Dragons. I pull out the character sheet I made with Dottie in study hall, and Kent Holt, who I'm sitting next to on one side (Henry somehow ended up on my other), pushes a *Player's Handbook* my way. "You'll probably need this. Or you can just ask me if you have questions. I have the book memorized." I flip through the golden-covered book in front of me and marvel at how someone could (and would) memorize the complicated text.

"So do I," Philip says, trying to sound impressive.

"Oh yeah? Then what script does the gnome language use?"

"Dwarven, duh."

Dottie interrupts, "Can you put away your geek dicks for a second so we can start playing?"

Philip grumbles, but Kent mouths to me, "I so know more than he does."

Dottie starts the adventure like a storyteller sharing a tale. "Your party wanders into a town square, elaborately decorated for what looks to be a celebration or festival."

"Is there a pub?" Eddie interrupts.

"Of course," Dottie answers. "A sign for the Leaky Bucket is visible from where you stand."

"To the Leaky Bucket!" Eddie cries.

"The Leaky Bucket!" repeats everyone else (me not included).

"Very well. You enter the Leaky Bucket."

"I order an ale," Eddie interrupts again.

"If you insist on interrupting the DM, you may soon find yourself struck blind by purple lightning." Eddie zips his lips with his finger.

The adventure continues like this for a good twenty minutes, with everyone eating and drinking at the pub, then having to choose a slice of pie from cherry, peach, or kumquat. Naturally I choose kumquat because the name's so great, as do Kent and Henry. Philip and Eddie choose cherry, and Doug peach. Dottie, who hides her head behind some strategically opened books standing upright on the table, picks up some dice and starts rolling. I look at Henry, but he just shrugs like he doesn't know what Dottie's doing. Then Dottie peeks her head over her blockade with a wicked grin. "Roll for initiative."

I whisper to my guru, Kent, "What does she mean 'roll for initiative'?"

"You're just rolling a twenty to see what order we go in."

"Order for what?"

"Something big. Whenever the DM says 'Roll for initiative,' you know something big is going to happen." Kent hands me a blue frosted, twenty-sided die (a "twenty") and tells me to roll.

"Fifteen," I say. "Is that good?"

Kent tries to explain that it's not good or bad necessarily, depending on when you want to go and where you want to be in the fight. I have no idea what he's talking about, but I nod so I don't look like an idiot. (I feel weird that *I'm* the idiot in this situation, being at a fake pub and all.) He complicates it even further by telling me to add my modifiers, but I figure out that if I just pause for second, he'll do it for me.

We go around the table and tell Dottie our initiative numbers. I'm embarrassed to say that my heart is beating heavily in my chest with anticipation. Will Imalthia have to fight? Could she get hurt? Could she hurt someone else? My excitement momentum is broken by the doorbell.

"Pizza!" cries Doug, and he stumbles out of his giant chair with the money in hand.

I call after him, "It's right on time, so you can give the guy all of it!"

"Are you like this in restaurants?' Henry asks me. "Timing the waiters and docking their tips if they don't show up fast enough?"

"Depends on how hungry I am."

Doug drops a stack of pizza boxes on the table. There's a mad dash for the pizza, but no one needs to worry since we ordered three extra larges. We pour our drinks, and when we're about settled, Dottie asks, "Are you ready to get hurt?"

"Ask your NPCs!" Philip cackles, and everyone (except me) laughs.

"Non-player characters," Kent tells me, which still makes no sense.

Henry explains, "NPCs are like the extras on a movie set. The Dungeon Master controls them, and we fight them or talk to them or steal from them, etc."

"Got it." I love the way Henry and Kent are helping me learn the game. It feels like they're protecting me from something. Kind of romantic. Except only from Henry. Not from Kent. At least I hope not.

Any romance I was feeling for all of two seconds has now turned to sheer violence. We're in a battle with a group of orcs that overheard us talking in the pub and didn't like us eating all of their kumquat pie. Everyone has their turn (initiative) to tell the DM what they want to do. We have to say which weapon we plan to use (if any), who we want to hit, and how we want to do it. Luckily I don't have to go first, and I listen to Philip's and Doug's turns. When Dottie gets to me, I'm pumped. Finally a fight!

"I take out my sword," I say, "and I go after orc number two." After that, I roll the twenty to see if I hit him. According to Dottie, my sixteen is high enough that I do, and then I get to roll. . . . I do, and then I get to roll another die to see how much damage I do to him. Everyone in the game has a certain number of hit points, which are like life points. When someone does damage to you, you lose hit points. If you lose enough of them, you can die.

We go around the table and take turns until all of the orcs are dead (except for one who runs away like a wuss). Most of us escaped unharmed, except for Eddie (who, Dottie informs me, my character accidentally hit with my sword when I rolled a one, the crappiest roll you can get).

"That was so fun," I can't help but announce to the table. "I am definitely playing again next week."

Everyone looks at me like I'm a freak. "We just got into a bar fight. We don't even know why we're in this town yet," Eddie snorts.

"No need to be a scrote, Eddie," Dottie comes to my defense. "She's never played before. She doesn't know."

"Yeah, you're just pissed 'cause she jacked you up." Philip laughs.

"Whatever. So what're we doing now?"

While Dottie continues her storytelling, Henry leans over and whispers, "You did great. Nice wielding of the sword." He bumps my shoulder with his. It was just a quick bump, so it probably didn't mean anything. Did I want it to?

I am completely immersed in the game, in my character,

Imalthia, when my cell phone goes off. It's Barrett, calling to say he's coming to pick me up now so he can go to bed because he has work tomorrow. I look at my cell phone and see it's 11:45. "I can't believe it's this late," I say.

"Yeah. I guess we should leave off here. Everyone's getting picked up at midnight, anyway," Henry says as he starts cleaning up half-empty cups and pizza boxes.

"Not me," Eddie sings.

"That's because you live next door, Eddie," Dottie deadpans.

I help stack books, return dice to their proper pouches, and carry the used plates and napkins into the kitchen. Dottie and Henry follow with the rest of the garbage. My cell phone rings, and I know that Barrett is outside waiting for me. "That's my brother," I tell the room. "I better go. Thanks so much for inviting me." I look at Dottie and then at Henry.

"No prob, girlfriend." Dottie sticks her hand out in a gesture to receive a five, and I smack her hand. "All right. So I'll see you in study hall, and we can discuss the possibility of costumes?"

My phone starts buzzing again, and I hurriedly leave the kitchen to shut it off. I call back to the kitchen, "See you guys at school! Thanks again," and to Philip, Eddie, and Kent, "See you guys. That was fun," and they mumble their good-byes as I step into the silent night air.

Barrett must have dropped Chloe off before he came to get

me because the front seat is empty. I slide in and buckle my seat belt. "Thanks for driving."

"No worries, mate," Barrett says. "Did you have a good time doing . . . whatever you were doing?" He eyes me suspiciously.

I think for a moment about the dice rolling, name calling, pizza eating, and the complete and total out-there-ness of the night. "Yeah," I finally declare, "I really did."

chapter 29

I SPEND SATURDAY WITH MOM,
going over pattern-making, just in case. I still haven't decided
whether I want to make the costumes for Fudwhalla, partly
because I'm afraid I'm not a good enough seamstress, but
mostly because of the fact that if I make those guys clothes, I
am definitely in. And I don't mean "in" in the way that "in" is
supposed to mean, which is what scares me. This is definitely
NOT the in-crowd or the A-List, but it might be a crowd I
want to be in. Not sure.

Mom teaches me to make a more elaborate style of skirt,
complete with pleats, longer, and lined. It takes us all day to
chalk the patterns onto the fabric (a dramatic purple velvet),
cut them out, and sew. When it's finished, the skirt looks semi-
professional, although the dark, brooding fabric may help hide
flaws. (Note to self *if* I sew the medieval costumes: Use dark
fabrics.)

My dad pops into my room while we sew. "So—sew?—So
how did it go last night? Slay any dragons? A beholder, perhaps? Come across any nymphs?" Dad gives me a cheesy,
knowing smile.

"Noooo," I elongate the word to keep him in suspense. Plus, I don't quite know what he's talking about (except for the dragon, duh). "Just some orcs. And I kind of chopped a member of our party." It almost feels like I'm bragging. Am I?

"Nice!" Dad drifts off into the fairyland in his head. "You're not looking for a middle-aged dwarven cleric, are you? I've got some great healing powers. . . ."

"Dad, it was just my first time with these guys. I think it's a bit premature for me to be inviting guests. Especially one of your advanced age."

"Ouch," Mom laughs. "I don't think I like the idea of you playing Dungeons and Dragons with a bunch of teenagers. Isn't that a bit icky?"

"Okay, okay. Maybe I'll just have to find a group of adventurers my own age." He playfully huffs out of the room.

"I really hope he's not serious," Mom says through clenched teeth where she holds two pins. She takes the pins carefully out of her mouth and stabs them into the pincushion tomato. "Better go start dinner. Chinese or Thai?"

Chinese food is always faster and the order is never wrong, but the Thai restaurant's food is better. "Thai," I say. "Cashew with tofu, please.

"Before you go, Mom, can I show you something?" She nods, and I pull open one of our ancient encyclopedias to a page I marked for costume ideas. "Do you think this would be hard to make?" The picture shows a man in tight pants and a flouncy shirt covered with some sort of vesty thing, and a woman in a corseted top worn over more flouncy sleeves and a very full, long skirt.

"Hmmm." Mom takes the book onto her lap and studies the picture. "The guy's outfit's easy. We could find a shirt like that, I'm sure, use a woman's if we have to. Buy some tights, and just sew a top to fit over the shirt. The woman's is harder, but now you know how to make a full skirt. We'd have to fudge the corset—I haven't really worked with underwire. Maybe we can try something with shoelaces?" She seriously considers our options, which is a little too committed for me.

"I was just wondering if it was possible. It's nothing." I think for a second that if I agree to make the costumes, I only have two weeks and now would be a great time to get started, but, "It's just something I'm thinking about."

"Well, let me know. I always love a good trip to the fabric shop." She kisses me on the head and says, "I'm very proud of you, honey. Your skirt is beautiful. They all are. A chip off the old mom." She beams, and leaves to "make" dinner.

Sunday morning, Barrett wakes me with a knock on my door. "Jess? You awake?" He pushes open my door with a composition notebook in his hands, and I dig the crust out of the corner of my eyes. Barrett drops onto my bed and bumps me upright. "Van's coming by today to pick up his drum kit."

"And I care why?" I ask, genuinely disgusted. I'm proud of myself for finally having that as my natural reaction to his name.

"I thought you might want one last jam session before they're gone?" I look at my clock. It's 8:15 A.M. I look back at Barrett and give a "What's the deal?" shrug. "Dickhead came to the movie theater yesterday with some unsuspecting chick on his arm. I've been putting off telling him about, *you know,* but I couldn't stand seeing him with another girl he might be diseasing. There was a line behind him, but he was picking his butt trying to decide between the five-dollar medium Coke or the $5.15 large, you know, being a cocky bastard. His girl, who looked way too young to be with him, was staring like a lovesick puppy at his smug face. I lost it."

"Did you hit him?" I ask excitedly. I picture Barrett leaping over the counter, punching the crap out of Van's too-gorgeous face.

"No. I didn't want to get fired. Not because of that chode. He took his sweet time, and I took the opportunity to introduce myself to the girl. Her name was Maddie, and she goes to Westgate High, and blah, blah—she went on and on with her bubbly crap. I finally interrupted and said, 'So, Maddie, did you know your boyfriend here has gonorrhea?' The kid looks confused, but Van, he's pissed and says, 'What the hell are you talking about?' And I say, real calm, so my manager doesn't suspect anything's up, 'Why don't you ask Bizza how her trip to the clinic went yesterday? And then have a visit yourself, *after*, of course, you call every other poor girl you've screwed over.' Van says, 'Bullshit. Bizza's just saying that 'cause I dumped her skinny ass and she's all boo-hoo about it.' I say, 'Sure, Van. Bizza's pretending to have gonorrhea to win you back. Such a turn-on, don't you agree, Maddie?' And Maddie just shakes her head in a disgusted no. Then Van tries to grab Maddie's arm, but she shakes him off and says something I don't hear. He's all huffy and walks off, so I yell after him, 'If you don't tell them, I will!' And he yells, 'Piss off,' and that he'll come get his drums today. So, yeah . . ." Barrett looks dreamily off into the distance with a satisfied smile.

"Do you think he's actually going to get himself checked out? And call those girls?" I can't imagine that if a guy is such a jerk that he won't even talk to a girl after she goes up to his bedroom, he's actually going to call a bunch of girls about giving them an STD.

"He'll go to a doctor for sure. He may be a selfish bastard, but his love for his johnson knows no bounds. Do I think he's going to call the girls? Probably not. But check this out." Barrett holds up the notebook. "Van's lyric book. He left it in the basement."

"What, did he write a song about every girl he screwed or something?" At this point I wouldn't put it past him.

"That shit-for-brains couldn't write a song to save his life. But he was quite thorough about other things." Barrett flips to a page toward the back of the book. Neatly numbered, starting with one and continuing all the way onto the next page, is a list of girls' names. "He kept track of every girl he ever hooked up with. I asked him once if he was having some sort of competition or something, but he said he did it so he didn't accidentally hook up with the same girl twice. He thought that would be wasteful."

"Yuck." I crinkle my nose.

"You said it. Anyway, we can definitely use this book if he isn't willing to do it himself." Barrett sounds unenthusiastic, hoping that calling Van's exes is something he won't have to do. "So—the basement in five minutes?" I nod and throw back the covers to get myself up. While I jump into my pajama pants, I think how I am so happy to be plain, straight-brown-haired girl and not buzzed, Van-attracting girl. It pisses me off that Van has such power over females, yet he's such a complete sleazoid creep. Not to mention I won't have any more drums to play.

Barrett tunes his guitar in the basement. I sit down behind Van's drum kit, the kit I learned to play on when me, Bizza, and Char started our band. Now Bizza's out of my life, Van's out of my head, and the drums will be no more. I kick the bass pedal hard. "Wait—are Mom and Dad up yet?"

"They've been up for hours. They're out to breakfast or on a hike or something. They left us donuts."

That is the invitation I need. Not the donuts, but the absence of anyone to annoy. I pound the bass pedal again, as hard as I can, so hard that the pedal buckles a bit under my foot.

"Hey, careful. You don't want to break the skin." He looks at me. I look back, eyebrows raised. "Or maybe you do?"

I'm barefoot in my pajamas, and run to get a pair of shoes. I scan the front hall closet and decide against canvas Chucks and leather flats. Instead, I choose the largest and heaviest pair of shoes I own: my winter boots. I slide them on over my pant legs as someone else takes over my brain. I'm Imalthia the fighter, and we're on a quest to defeat the evil scum of Van and stop his torment of women. I clomp down the basement steps. Barrett sees me and laughs. "You look a little remedial," he says. Imalthia growls at him, and he puts his hands up in surrender.

"Ready to jam?" Imalthia asks, a violent gleam in her eyes.

"Ready, Boots," Barrett answers. I tack my sticks together. One. Two. One-two-three-four, but instead of slapping the heads with my sticks, Imalthia jams the sticks directly down and through the drum pad. I pause and look up at Barrett, who holds his breath. Crash! I slam a cymbal then pummel another drum until I plunge the stick through. And then I do it again, and again, all very rhythmically, of course, until I get to the grand finale, the pièce de résistance, and I stand up and plow my winter-boot-covered foot through the bass drum.

I'm breathing heavily, and I realize my song has no guitar accompaniment. Barrett looks at me, a mix of shock and admiration. Then he declares, "You effed those drums up! Right on, sister!" And just like that, Imalthia is gone, and I'm standing in the basement in front of a destroyed drum kit, wearing my pajamas and winter boots. My mouth is a perfect O of disbelief.

"Mother of turds," I say. "He's gonna be pissed."

"And? He deserves it. He never plays them anymore, anyway. But maybe you should hide in your room when you hear the doorbell ring, just in case."

We abandon our jam session and head up to the kitchen for some donuts. I start out with the strawberry frosted and finish with the sprinkles. I feel jazzed, vindicated, like I don't need any of those jerks who made it so complicated to be friends. It is so much easier and so much more fun to be around people who include me—and not just for selfish reasons.

When the clock actually says it's a normal hour to be awake on a Sunday, I have a phone call to make.

chapter 30

TO KILL TIME UNTIL TEN O'CLOCK (the civilized hour whence to call someone on a Sunday), I shower and shave (my legs, that is), and work on some sketches for the costumes. I'm no artist, not like some of those designers who can draw fantastically stylized and funky images of their latest fashion lines. I don't actually know what I'm designing for, and there's a tiny part of me that worries they may have changed their minds, but what the heck.

I have the school directory open to the correct page, and I have efficiently punched the numbers into my phone so when the clock strikes (glows, technically) 10:00, I'll be ready. The longest minute of the day is excruciatingly 9:59, and during that minute my mind rushes through too many thoughts. *What are you doing? Are you really going to commit to this? Does wanting to do this make you one of them? Doesn't the fact that I want to hang out with them already make me one of them? What if they actually reject me? How pathetic would that be? What are you doing?* And then it's 10:00, and my finger automatically presses SEND. The phone rings, and:

"Heyyy," a slow, sleepy voice answers. "Hey" implies that

the person on the other end knows who's speaking, and yet I don't want to assume—ass out of you and me and whatnot.

"Hi, Dottie? It's Jessie. Sloan. From study hall?"

"Yeah, I know who it is. That's the glory of caller ID. And I know who you are, Jessie. We hung out all Friday night, remember?"

I don't know why I'm being so flubbedy, but it's always awkward when you talk to someone on the phone for the first time. Why is this such a big deal? I mean, it's Dottie Bell. The school's biggest . . .

"To what do I owe this early-morning call?" Dottie yawns into the phone. Maybe I should have waited until 10:30. If she didn't want to talk, she didn't have to answer the phone. Calm. Down. I'm not trying to impress anyone here.

I get it together. "I just called to say thanks for inviting me to D&D on Friday. It was really fun."

"Sure, sure. Hope to see you there next week, too. The party has way too much magic, not enough muscle without you." That makes me laugh a little because of how nonmuscular I actually am. Although, give me a pair of winter boots, and who knows what might happen.

"Definitely. I'd love to come."

"Cool." There's a long silence, and I wonder if Dottie has fallen back asleep or if she is doing something obscure on the other end, like dyeing her own wool or translating the Rosetta Stone.

"Hey, Dottie? About the costumes . . ."

"Yeah?" She suddenly perks up, and I get excited to tell her.

"I want to do it. I think it'll be fun. But there's not a lot of time, so—"

"Don't say another word. Me and the guys will be over later today to discuss our needs and for you to get measurements. Will you be home?"

Do I have a choice? "Yeah. I'll be here." And so will Barrett, I think, and he'll see my new group of friends in all their nerdly glory.

"Sweet. We'll get there after lunchtime. We have to wait till Eddie gets back from church." Eddie at church? Interesting.

We hang up, and I'm edgy. I really want to tell Barrett what I'm doing, but I'm afraid he's going to laugh. I'd laugh at him if he started hanging out with the senior geeks, right? Or would I? It's just as weird that Mr. Punk Rock King of Greenville High is now dating the most popular girl in school. Just because she's popular doesn't make her better than Barrett, and just because he's punk doesn't make him better than me. Or does it? Because punk is cool? And nerds aren't? I don't know why, but I wonder what Bizza and Char would say if they saw the D&D crew show up on my doorstep. Char would probably be polite and then laugh when they left. Bizza, on the other hand, would greet them with a "What up, dork fest?" to their faces. But then maybe she'd decide it's *subversive* to hang out with the uncool, and she'd make it her phase for all of three days until she got sick of them not worshipping her and—stop. Bizza and Char aren't part of this equation. They're not even part of this assignment or chapter. Hell, they'd never even get into the class. But Barrett's pretty smart. Maybe he'll get it.

Barrett has no idea what time Van will stop by, so the two of us spend late morning/early afternoon making grilled cheeses in our Sandwich Maker. The Sandwich Maker is perhaps the greatest invention of all time (yes, better than sliced bread, because I *could* slice the bread myself if necessary). All you have to do is make a sandwich like you'd normally make a grilled cheese, butter sides out, and once the Sandwich Maker is warmed up (indicated by the magical red glow on its lid), you open it up, place your sandwiches inside (lined up in the designated sandwich areas) and a couple of minutes later— voilà! (Or *viola*, as Bizza would incorrectly say)—you have two grilled cheeses, perfectly sealed on all four sides and divided into triangularly tasty halves. Genius!

When we finish lunch, I set up shop at the coffee table with my homework, starting with precalc. Barrett heads to the basement to disassemble Van's drum kit, so he can get it out of the house as quickly as possible once Van arrives. Barrett claims he's not worried about dealing with Van, and he would even be a little happy if he's forced to, as he put it, "Beat Van's ass." That doesn't stop me from worrying, but I suppose I'm technically off the hook until Van actually heads to the basement. Not that I want to greet him at the front door.

The doorbell rings, and I jump. I try to compose myself in case Van reads the mix of fear and guilt on my face, but instead I see Henry's face peek into one of the windows near the front door. Behind him, I see Philip and Kent. A giant grin involuntarily explodes across my face. I'm so happy it's them and not Van.

Before I can open the front door, Barrett comes pounding up the basement stairs. "I'll get it!" he yells, and pushes me aside to yank open the front door. There stands the whole Dungeons and Dragons crew: Dottie, Doug, Kent, Philip, Eddie, and Henry (who, I note, is wearing a different pair of long pants than the other day, this time black cords). "Can I . . . help you?" Barrett asks in confusion.

"They're here for me, Barrett," I say, trying not to hesitate for their benefit.

"Really?" he asks, and I'm not sure if he's confused or condescending. I nod and invite everyone in.

Politely Henry asks, "Should we remove our shoes?" So different from the boot brigade of Char and Bizza.

"Not unless you stepped in dog poop," I say. "You can just wipe them on the mat." And a thundering cavalcade of wiping ensues.

"Aren't you going to introduce me?" Barrett asks, and I'm

ready to snap at him for the sarcasm or irony I expect in his voice, but there is none. Barrett has a welcoming smile on his face that screams interested big brother.

"Okay. Um, everyone, this is my brother, Barrett." A chorus of his, heys, and nice-to-meet-yous follow. I introduce each person by first and last name, and each of them, initiated by Dottie, sticks out a hand for a handshake. I'm kind of in awe. I don't know why I assumed Barrett would intimidate a group of people who have absolutely no idea who he is, nor why Barrett, who barely knew any of these guys existed before today, would judge them all. What's even more amazing is the confidence that Dottie and her friends project—the friendly handshake, the genial eye contact—instead of the aloof toughness of the punk crowd or the snotty snubs of the popular crowd.

"And how do you guys know each other?" Barrett asks. He couldn't just have left it at hello?

I intervene before anyone else can jump in. "Well, I know Dottie from study hall, and these guys through her." All true.

"We played Dungeons and Dragons on Friday night," Eddie blurts.

Thank you, Eddie. Didn't they teach you at church *thou shalt not blab*?

"Aaah." Barrett looks at me with a lightbulb flicking on above his head. "Friday night . . ." He turns back to the group and says something that utterly shocks me. "I tried D&D once in junior high." What? "It was a little too complex for my lazy ass, but it seemed pretty cool." The group nods with what I detect to be pride, and I'm speechless. Why didn't I know about this? Was Barrett embarrassed or was I just too young to care?

I don't exactly know how to end this bizarre conversion of the social strata until I see Van's crappy car pull into the driveway.

"Why don't we go upstairs to my room and I'll show you my ideas?" I quickly usher everyone up the stairs, but not before Van walks through the front door as a witness. I hear his obnoxious voice ask, "What's happening here?"

"Jessie just has some friends over," Barrett explains, and their voices are lost as they head to the basement and I head to my room. Some *friends*. Not kids from school. Not weirdos or dorks or nerds. Friends.

It didn't occur to me earlier that I would be having a group of people in my bedroom. Luckily, I'm a relatively neat person. No undies or bras lying about, and only a few Rupert Grint pictures that could be slightly incriminating. The only messy area is my sewing table, and that's not too bad, just some scraps of fabric and empty bobbins.

No one except Dottie attempts to sit on my bed, which seems really sweet of the guys, but I feel guilty that everyone's piled onto the floor. I throw my comforter over my pillows so it's covering my sheets, and invite people to sit. I also pull out my sewing chair and footstool. When everyone's comfy, I find them looking up at me in anticipation. I am not used to people giving me this kind of attention.

"The first thing I need to know is what you're looking for. I mean, I can't make, like, leather armor or chain mail. It has to be simple. Because I'm not that good, and we don't have that much time. When exactly is it again?"

"Two weeks from yesterday," Dottie says.

"And what exactly is it again?"

Kent explains, "It's sort of like we are actually in a D&D adventure, like we're actually our characters. There's a whole town set up in a Wisconsin field, and we're sort of like actors, only we make up our own lines."

"Will there be, like, magic and fighting and stuff?" I question.

"Not for real." Kent laughs, thank god. "But some of us will have swords. You can have one if you want. But they'll be wooden and we won't technically fight with them. We'll just pretend that we do."

I rewind past the fighting and repeat, "Me included?" I hadn't thought about going to this thing. I thought I was just the royal seamstress.

"Yeah, I mean, if you want to be a fighter."

"I see Jessie as more of a chamber maid at Fudwhalla. No offense, Jess. That way she can follow my lead and won't get into trouble." Dottie has obviously thought this through. I am still stuck on how they're so willingly including me in this thing.

"Wait—so I would go with you? And be a chamber maid? Is that like a toilet maid?"

Dottie laughs her low chuckle. "Kind of, although there won't be any real toilets where we're going." Everyone laughs like they're sharing some toiletless memory. "You'd be like my lady-in-waiting." Then Dottie explains that there is actually a preplanned plot to Fudwhalla, where Dottie and Doug are a baroness and barron, and the guys are all some kind of knight or spy or manservant. And there will be a whole bunch of other people there, too, in on the game, each with a different part to play. It almost sounds like live theater without an audience. "So no toilets?" I double-check. "Where do we sleep?"

"We'll all bring sleeping bags, but we get to sleep inside a little royal house they make for us," Dottie continues. "And there's a dining hall, and fake money, and weird little stands where people sell all kinds of jewelry and snacks and fake wooden weapons. Oh—that reminds me. We have to pay Nigel before next Friday." Nigel?

"Nigel's the guy running this whole thing. He's a totally medieval-obsessed dork, but we went to Fudwhalla last year, and it was quite professional. You'll have fun."

There isn't even a question at this point of whether or not I'm going, which is nice because they want me with them, but frightening because this sounds completely out of my comfort zone. Bizza and Char and I never did anything like this. The closest thing was camping out for half a night in my backyard so we could study the constellations during our astrology phase. But we went inside around two A.M. when Char got assaulted with mosquito bites because she refused to spray herself with DEET in case it stained her clothes. And then there's my own personal camping nightmare.

"I'm not exactly the world's best camper," I admit, not wanting to repeat the time I camped with my family and had to poo in the woods in the middle of the night. I was too afraid that a bear would eat me (thanks to Barrett's grizzly campfire tales), so I ended up pooing in my pants and stinking up the tent for the rest of the trip. It was so nasty, Barrett and I ended up sleeping in the car. Not that I'm actually that afraid of bears anymore or that I think I'll poop in my pants in the middle of the night, but there are just too many stinky memories.

"How long does Fudwhalla last?" I ask.

"Saturday morning until Sunday afternoon's banquet," Henry answers.

"And we'll be in a house?"

"Yeah, kind of. They're what you'd call bare-bones structures. But they're not tents," Doug explains.

"And we won't actually be fighting?"

"Only if you're fighting off the advances of the other royal's hired help," Dottie smirks.

"We'll keep you safe, ma'am," Henry assures me.

How can I say no to all of this? They're including me in

this huge weekend thing that they've already done once together as a group. Just like that. I'm completely nervous, but I
look around the room at their nerdy, goofy, and even cute
faces, and know that I'll be taken care of. It's been a long time
since I felt this way with Bizza and Char, and Barrett won't be
around much longer to big-brother me.

"Let's plan the costumes," I say, and we get into it. I learn
that the costumes don't have to be historically accurate, seeing
as we're not actually reenacting part of history. We can fudge
a lot of it with what we already own, and they just need me to
come up with a unifying tunic for the men to wear and some
sort of skirt for us womenfolk. I tell Dottie about the big
skirts, and she seems really excited (or, as excited as supermel-
low Dottie gets). I have to measure all of the guys on top
(thank god I'm not sewing any pants), and it's funny to watch
Kent suck in his gut as I bring the tape measure from around
his back.

"Kent," I say, "the tunic's not going to fit you if you suck
it in. Let it all hang out." And he does.

When I get to Henry, it's a little more complicated than
with the other guys. I avoided a Henry dream last night, so it
could have been worse, but I can't help but notice his solid
stomach as I bring around the tape measure, or the broadness
of his shoulders. I didn't ask anyone to take off their shirts
(Mostly because these are just going to be loose-fitting tunics
anyway, but partially because I didn't want to have to see Kent
or Eddie without shirts. And they seemed grateful when I told

them they could keep their shirts on). Being this close to Henry shirted, well, is my mind really going there?

Dottie and I decide to go to the fabric store tomorrow after school and then collect money from everyone after we see how much it will cost.

I walk the crew out when we're finished, and I'm surprised when they each give me a friendly hug along with an enthusiastic thank-you for making the costumes. My parents come in from the garage just as I close the front door.

"Hiya, Jess. Who just left?"

"Hi, Dad. Those were my friends," I tell him.

The day had turned out to be so fun and easy that I almost forgot about Van and the drum kit. He was long gone when everyone left. I didn't want to ask Barrett about it at dinner in case my parents would lay some guilt on me about the destruction of someone else's property, so I wait until he's getting ready for bed.

"So?" I ask.

"So what?" he says through a mouthful of toothpaste foam.

"What happened with Van?" I demand. My adrenaline is pumping, like I'm ready for a fight if Van wants to start one. I can just see us at the bike racks after school.

Barrett spits into the sink and runs the water, taking his

time so he can keep me in suspense as long as possible. So obnoxious, yet so predictable. He's about to floss when I kick his slippered foot with mine. Barrett finally spills, "Well, I wish you could've been there. I was totally ready for him to blow up when I told him I had his book and was going to use it to call all of those girls if he didn't."

"What did he say?" I sit on the toilet (grateful for a lid) and rest my elbow on the sink, chin in hand, looking up at Barrett.

"He grumbled that he'd call them, but I said I'd keep the book for a while just in case. You and I can check up on some of the names to see if he's calling."

"That'll be fun," I smirk. "And the drums?" I'm practically vibrating with excitement at the thought of Van's discovery of the explosion-like holes in his drum kit.

"Oh, that was hilarious. He was so trying so hard just to be cool. I saw him stop, though, and his mouth puckered a little like he just sucked on some deodorant. Classic." Barrett laughs to himself at the memory, continuing to heighten my anticipation of the big moment. "And then . . ." Yes? Yes? "Then he started taking apart the kit and carrying it piece by piece to his car."

"And then what?" There has to be more.

"And then he said, 'Later,' no eye contact or friendly handshake, of course, and left." Barrett folds his hands across his chest and looks down at me.

"That's it? He wasn't even mad?" I'm shocked.

"I'm sure he was mad, but what could he say? He knew I had a million things to be pissed at him about, plus I had his notebook. Maybe a part of him thought he deserved it."

Weird, but possible. And it's not like he was that attached to his drum kit, considering it had been at our house for the last three years. I can't say I'm not a little disappointed that there wasn't more of a fight, because Van so deserves to have his ass kicked. But when I think about how many girls he has to call and tell he might have given them gonorrhea . . . Maybe he's saving his fighting for that.

chapter 31

THE SCHOOL WEEK PASSES IN SUCH
a mild-mannered way that it almost makes up for the assiness
of the beginning of the year. I see Van a couple of times in
the hallway, but he passes by with no acknowledgment. I at
least hope he's trying to ignore me and not that he truly
doesn't notice me. I'd like to think I've got more effect on
him than that at this point. Char gives me a half-assed
friendly wave but never stops to chat when I see her (not that
I stop either). I catch glimpses of Bizza here and there, back
to her dramatic punk look, but she seems to be avoiding me
because we haven't actually passed in the halls all week. It's
pretty sweet that I'm not the one having to do the avoiding
anymore.

I spend my lunch hours with the band geeks, who I'd feel
bitchy dropping altogether since they were so amazingly welcoming when I needed it. Besides, the only D&D person in
my lunch hour is Henry, and I'm trying to keep my cool. Not
truly consciously, but I'm worried that the more time I spend
with him, the more I'll like him. Stupid, I know, because there

really shouldn't be anything wrong with liking him. But the jerky part of my brain thinks otherwise.

Dottie and I buy fabric for the costumes on Monday after school, and I rush home each day to sew. I only have this week, this weekend, and next week before we leave for Fudwhalla on that Saturday morning. My parents were perfectly willing to let me go, particularly after Barrett noted, "No worries, guys. Jessie's nerd herd will take good care of her." I thought we were beyond name-calling after yesterday. I guess Barrett was just being polite. I can't say I'm not disappointed. But it's not like I'm one hundred percent past the labeling either.

It's Friday, and I wonder whether Henry will remember about our Friday lunch going-out thing (*not* a date). I debate pretending to forget, but I hate when other people forget things *and* I hate lying. I rarely forget things. My wonders and worries are answered when I see Henry in the hall before second-period gym. Until this morning, I had managed to keep him out of my dreams (and I won't go into detail of the very graphic nature of today's pre-alarm-clock fandango), but now I'm all fidgety with Henry confusion. He looks cute, too, with his full-length pants and a Batman T-shirt I remember seeing at Target. It's somewhat fitted and shows off his decidedly un-nerdy chest and arms. He smiles at me in a completely comfortable, nonflirty way, and I wonder why I had any worry at all about seeing him. He confirms that "We're on" for lunch today and reminds me that I'm buying.

As I trudge around the track during gym, I'm surprised at how I feel a little disappointed about the undateness of the whole thing. Would Henry be different to me in a different universe? All twisty hair and scorching eyes? But *this* is the universe I'm in, so I need to figure this out on my own plane.

Lunch today is as pleasant as it was last week, with held-open doors, multiple burgers, and excellent, easy conversation. I am completely hung up on the nondate thing when I do something unexpected (even to me, which is weird since I'm the one doing it). After we're done eating and it's time to cross the street, I remember how Henry grabbed my hand last time to help me across. I decide (and this is the unexpected part) not to wait for Henry, or even for when the time comes to cross the street, but to grab his hand preemptively. So I do. We stand there, on the wrong side of the street, holding hands until a very clear break in the traffic forces us to cross, still holding hands. And we keep holding hands all the way up to the school doors, when Henry lets go to hold a door open for me. The bell rings, and we both hurriedly separate and yell, "See you tonight!"

All I can think about during precalc is how warm and perfect it felt to hold Henry's hand and how terrified I am that I'll feel that way again.

chapter 32

IT TURNS OUT DUNGEONS AND
Dragons is at Henry's house almost every Friday night, due to
his parents' active social life and, as Kent explained, "His fancy
chairs set a good mood for the game." Is it weird that I totally
know what he means?

I end up sitting between Henry and Kent again, which I'm
glad about so I don't have to avoid (or attempt) eye contact
with Henry the whole night, but not glad about because there's
always the possibility of touching his masculine veiny (but not
in a gross, steroid way) forearm.

The vibe is happy, with even Eddie lightening up on me
because of the costumes. We pause from the game for a while
when the pizzas arrive (our party was in the middle of trying
to disarm some traps around a mysterious cabin in the woods).
Kent and Doug are discussing highlights from last year's Fudwhalla.

"Remember that guy with the giant—"

"That was hilarious! And that girl with the thing—"

"Totally!" Pizza bits fly everywhere, but I don't gain any

more understanding of what I'm in for next weekend. Dottie calls me over to sit beside her.

"Jess, guess what I found in my mom's forbidden drawer."

Did she really want me to guess? The lengthy pause tells me yes. "Um, handcuffs?" I guess because that seems like something that might be in a forbidden drawer.

"That, too, but come here and I'll show you." Dottie leads me into the foyer while the guys eat. She rifles through a giant messenger bag and pulls out two elaborately lacy and ribboned corsets. "Score, right?" I can only look at her and pray she doesn't hand one to me. Apparently, I'm not quick enough on the prayers because she thrusts a black corset, intricately woven throughout with lavender ribbon, into my hand. "I'm keeping the one with red ribbons because it has more padding. I don't think you need it." To say it's disturbing that Dottie has thought about if I needed padding would be undermining the fact that she wants me to wear her mom's corset.

"Dottie—I can't wear this. Your mom's boobs touched it."

Dottie snorts, "I wouldn't do that to you, Jess. The tags are still on, see? My mom just buys this stuff in case the mood hits. She has drawers of it, complete with tags." I double-check, and thankfully the tags are still intact. But a corset?

"When exactly do you want me to wear this?" Visions dance through my head of a surprise after-pizza dual strip-tease performance.

"For Fudwhalla, duh. We can wear them over our blouses. They'll look great with the skirts you're making." Dottie and I decided that I would sew full skirts, and she would take care of the top half. I guess it won't be too bad if we're wearing them over our shirts.

I stuff the corset into my bag so no one sees, even though it would not technically be seeing my underwear (because it would technically be seeing Dottie's mom's underwear). I really hope this doesn't mean the guys will be wearing jockstraps over their pants.

When the pizza boxes have been thoroughly demolished, we continue our adventure. I say we should try breaking through a window near the back of the cabin. Dottie merrily sneers and commands, "Roll for initiative." A chorus of "Shits" and "Nice going, Imalthia" round the table. "What?" I question. "It doesn't mean something bad is going to happen, it just means *something* is going to happen. And it's better than standing around picking our butts in the woods all day. Unless you enjoy that sort of thing, Eddie," I add onto the end.

"Watch it, n00b," he threatens, but I know he's just kidding.

The adventure gets really exciting and violent at this point, and midnight rolls around way too quickly. We decide to forget D&D next Friday for a costume fitting and an early night's sleep. Fudwhalla is an hour's drive, and we need to get there early to set up our "Place of Residence," as Kent calls it. I'm freaked about spending an entire weekend with a group of new friends and a whole lot of men in tights, not to mention SLEEPING near all of them. What if they snore? What if *I* snore? What if I fart in my sleep? What if I have to poo in the woods in the middle of the night? What if—

My panicked thoughts are interrupted by a strong hand on my shoulder and Henry's voice in my ear. "Your brother's here, Jessie." His eyes are Nalgene bottle blue tonight. I wish I could be as relaxed around him as he is around me. I wish my pervy dreams and overactive brain would leave me alone. I wish . . . I wish he and I were the only ones in the room right now.

Barrett's horn honks, and I quickly gather my stuff, careful not to let the corset accidentally peek out of my bag. When I get home, I decide to store the corset in the bottom of my never-wear-but-too-sentimental-to-get-rid-of T-shirt drawer. But first I absolutely have to try it on. I lock my door, take the corset out of my bag, then double-check to make sure the door is still locked. I take off my shirt, then my bra, then check the lock one more time with my hands over my chest. Still locked. I examine the corset and am happy to discover that instead of having to lace it up, as I've seen done in countless period movies, there's a hidden zipper on the side. The crisscrossed ribbons are just for show. I bring the zipper around the front, zip it up, and then turn the corset so it's on correctly. It's tight. The zipper is surrounded by elastic, but it's definitely snug. My boobs are smashed down below the plunging sweetheart neckline, and I delicately reach in and pull them out so they're sort of sitting within the supportive cups sewn inside. I look in the mirror and am in awe of my cleavage, which is now dangerously close to attacking my neck. I put my hands on my hips and think, *Hey, not bad.* There is my blah brown hair, though, so I jam my fingers in and shake it. It falls slightly less flat, and I'm about to try flinging it forward for even more height when I realize the corset doesn't exactly allow for forward motion. I unzip it and place it carefully in its hiding place. As I fall asleep, I wonder what Henry will think of all of this. I awake the next morning to faint dream memories of corsets and jockstraps.

chapter 33

THE WEEKEND IS A BLUR OF FAB-
ric and thread. By Sunday night, I'm almost finished with the
skirts (I made them before I made the guys' things so I can
perfect my corseted self before next weekend). That leaves me
with five tunics to sew by Friday. The panic sets in, but I have
to put aside the sewing for a bit of homework. This is a particularly brutal week for quizzes and tests. (Why do teachers
do that? Is it some teacherly conspiracy to put students over
the edge? Are they sitting in the teachers' lounge evilly laughing about it right now?) I'm in the middle of (what else?) precalc homework, when Barrett busts into my bedroom.

"Read this." He shoves a sloppy stack of papers on top of
my precalc book.

"What is it?"

"It's my NYU early admission essay. I have to send it in
by November first, so I want to make sure it's perfect. Will
you read it?"

His electric excitement almost eclipses the reality of him
going away to college. I look down at the papers. "Is it okay if

I read them later? I kind of put off my homework for the weekend until now." He deflates and tries to take the papers off my desk. "Leave them," I say. "Maybe I'll have a little time after my math homework." He perks up a bit and kisses the top of my head before he leaves my room. It's very rare that Barrett kisses me, and for a second I almost think he may feel a little sad about leaving.

Doubtful.

By 11:30, I have completed all of tomorrow's assignments and outlined my English short essay for Friday. Barrett's application sits tauntingly on the corner of my desk, and I think about leaving it there until he asks me about it again but know that he'll for sure ask again first thing in the morning. Might as well read it now.

I snuggle down in my bed with my trusty lightweight book light flopping over the loose pages of Barrett's application. Several of the pages are short essay or fill-in-the-blank Social Security number type questions, and I decide I'll leave those until later. The part everyone always freaks about is the essay, and it seems like it would make much more interesting reading than a list of Barrett's accomplishments and grade point average. Barrett's essay choice is A, to write about a person, place, or event that has meaning and why it is important. My mind races for a minute, thinking about how I might answer the question, but my droopy eyelids convince me to read Barrett's essay before I fall asleep. I wouldn't want to have to wake myself even earlier in the morning in order to read his essay (I never know what kind of dream I may be interrupting).

Barrett's essay begins:

As someone who has always considered himself a leader, I have a major distaste for followers. Followers are particularly obvious in what is known to many as the "popular" or "in-crowd." Some people spend their entire school careers trying to be liked and to fit in with a group that doesn't even want them. But the popular clique isn't the only group with followers; many of the fringe groups have them as well. For the last four years I have been immersed in the local punk scene. I have definitely seen my share of followers, poseurs, and wannabes. Sometimes it's hard to weed out the genuinely interesting people from those who just desperately want to be liked. I'm not immune to the guile of the try-hards, but there is one person in my life who has consistently reminded me how unimportant it is to do what everyone expects you to do—my sister, Jessie.

Did I just read what I think I read? I scan the page and see my name peppered throughout. I reread the opening paragraph and confirm that he's talking about me, then skim the rest of the page, too tired to read it thoroughly. I catch snippets:

. . . such a natural talent, learning the drums and adopting an unfamiliar style of music . . .

. . . her distinctive fashion sense; Jessie designs and sews her own skirts.

But the line I'm most drawn to is

I admire how she fearlessly dumped her user friends for a new group of oddballs.

I put the essay down. I don't know whether to feel flattered or offended. Of course, it's way flattering that my brother, whom I have always looked up to and adored, would make the focus of his precious college essay about me. But his basic thesis is that I made friends with a bunch of dorks. It's all well and good that he "admires" me for that, but he's the one who went from freaky to preppy in the span of a month. Sure, it's "cool" in theory to be friendly to nerds, but it's another thing entirely to be seen as one of them. And that's how Barrett sees me.

I angrily toss my book light on the floor and then worry that I busted it. More fun is tossing Barrett's college application, which makes a pleasantly violent sound as it cracks through the air and lands scattered around my floor.

My alarm wakes me Monday morning from a bizarre dream: I'm in my bedroom, only it's not quite my bedroom. The closet is in a different place, and my pictures of Rupert Grint are gone. As I walk through the room, it sounds like I'm stepping on autumn leaves, but when I look down I see the floor is covered with papers with the word "Jessie" in big black letters and the word "REJECTED" stamped across everything in red. I go to my wrongly placed closet door (Why are rooms in dreams never exactly the way they are in real life? Is this where my subconscious wants my closet door to be?), open it, and a million gray bats fly out at me, each with a tiny Lord of the Rings symbol glowing on their stomachs.

That's when I woke up. I prefer the Henry dreams, even if I'm not sure if I want them.

I get out of bed and step directly onto a piece of paper— Barrett's application. Oh yeah. The essay. It's amazing how a dream about Lord of the Rings bats can make you forget.

I get ready for school in a huff, locking the bathroom door to prevent any unexpected Barrett intrusions. I don't know what to say to him. Did he really think I could just read the essay objectively to let him know if I think it'll get him into NYU? Or was he expecting me to get all weepy at his generosity of including me in such an important piece of his life?

I avoid breakfast by yelling down to the fam that I'm finishing a skirt. I consider making up some other excuse to get out of driving to school with Barrett, but he sabotages my thoughts by barging into my room. My floor is covered with his essay, and I panic a little that he'll be mad at me for not being more careful. Then I remember I'm the one who should be mad, and besides that, a few papers on my floor could never compare to the piles of crap in his room. He doesn't even notice, just bounds over to me as I sit on my bed and asks, "Did you read it? What did you think?" His pathetically eager expression softens me a bit. I wish I didn't have to be angry.

"What did you want me to think?" I ask him, a little too snottily.

"I thought you'd like it." He hesitates. "You didn't?"

"Oh yeah, everyone loves being called a dork, Barrett. Not that you'd know."

He looks really confused, and I have the urge to slap the look off his perfect face. "I didn't call you a dork. I mean, I did, but it wasn't in a bad way."

"You said I dumped my friends for a bunch of outcasts and nerds!" I yell.

"That's not what I said, Jess. Not exactly. Did you read the whole essay?"

"Nooo," I say, afraid this is about to turn into some cheesy sitcom situation where one person thinks they hear someone say something but really they said something else, then absurd situations occur and laughter ensues.

"Where is it? I'll show you." My hand directs him, game-show-hostess style, across my bedroom floor. "Nice, Jess," he says as he picks up the crumpled sheets and shuffles through them. "Here, read the last line."

I dramatically grab the page from him and scan down to the end of the essay. I read, *Jessie is my inspiration, and I hope I am fortunate enough to find friends just as fun, unique, and cre-ative as Jessie has, without caring about what others think, should I be accepted at New York University.*

Wait. Did that just say I'm Barrett's inspiration? That he wishes he could find friends like mine? That I don't care what other people think? If he only knew.

"I was saying good things about you, Jess. Great, in fact. I think it's really cool how you found a new group of people to hang out with."

"Just the other day you called them nerds."

"No I didn't!"

"You totally did. You said to mom and dad that I'd be okay going to Fudwhalla because I'd be safe with, and I quote, my 'nerd herd.' I know you used the word 'nerds.' "

"I don't know. Force of habit, I guess. But nerd doesn't have to be a bad word. Can't it just be a social scene, like punk or goth? Like, 'Hey, I'm part of the nerd scene at Greenville High.' "

Barrett is trying to charm me, but it's just annoying.

"If you think being a nerd is so cool, why are you going out with Chloe Romano?"

"Jess, I can't change the fact that I like someone. Who can? I promise when I go off to college I'll try and date someone geekier. Like a math major or—"

"Watch it. I might be a math major someday. And what happened to marrying Chloe?" Even though it goes against my whole nerd pride speech, it's pretty hard not to approve of Chloe.

215

"She wants to take it slow. She says it's only October, and she wants to go to school in California." He flicks a loose thread on my comforter.

"It didn't look like she wanted to take it slow on the couch the other night."

"Slow in the serious relationship sense. Not the couch sense. I'm still hoping to bring her around, though." He looks up. "So you get it, Jess? That essay is about how much you amaze me. My little sister, who I always wanted to look up to *me*, has me looking up to her." He touches the tip of his finger to my nose and just keeps it there. I whack it off.

"I guess it's okay, then," I say.

"What's okay?"

"Your essay. I mean, it's good. Very moving. Hopefully a nerd will be reading it in the admissions office. Then you'll definitely be in."

"Yessss. So you give it the nerd stamp of approval?" He pauses and looks mortified that he just said that, and my insides cringe. But after his essay and everything that has happened in the last few weeks, I decide it's time to admit something.

I raise my fist and pound it on top of his application like a stamp. "Approved," I declare.

chapter 34

I LEAVE FOR SCHOOL FEELING GREAT on Monday morning, and the glow continues all week. I ace exams all over the place (thanks to some lunchtime study sessions with Henry), work on the Fudwhalla costumes at night, and even squeeze in a little audiobook time in my afternoon walks home.

Char has left three messages and six texts on my cell, just to say hi and see what's up. I send a neutral text reply, *BAU* [Business as usual]. *Skool keeping me bzy. TTYLR.* And I think I will talk to her later. Just not yet. And Bizza, I'm not so sure.

My skirts reflect my good mood, and I have worn a different skirt each day from what I call my "circus collection," which includes a variety of clown, animal, and snack prints. Friday I put on a red skirt covered in popcorn boxes, kernels, and the word "pop!" (This skirt can be cross-referenced with my "movie collection.")

In English, I'm about to plug into my iPod to listen to *Harry Potter and the Sorcerer's Stone* (audiobook comfort food) when Polly passes me a note.

Polly: Where've you been at lunch? We miss you.

Chip keeps insisting that you're off having some lunchtime affair with that student teacher from the drama department.

Me: Gross. And anyway, I heard he was having an affair with Mr. Zapata from shop. I've just been studying in the library. Sorry to disappoint.

Polly: Please come back. Chip's stories get more and more graphic. You don't actually own any leopard-print lingerie, do you?

Me: If I did, would I tell Chip?

Polly: True. You'll be there today?

Me: Have plans. But definitely Monday.

Polly: Doing anything this weekend?

I'd actually really like to tell Polly all about Fudwhalla, but it's way too complicated to pass in a note. I can tell her all about it next week at lunch after the fact.

Me: Yeah—camping with friends. A little role-playing action.

Polly: Ooh—like sexy role-playing? Or hack and slash role-playing?

Me: The 2nd. But if you want to tell Chip otherwise, be my guest.

Polly: Maybe we shouldn't feed his masturbatory fantasies.

Polly and I laugh, and Ms. Norton gives us the international symbol for shush.

I put in my earbuds and press PLAY, but my mind wanders to this weekend. It's going to be crazy—costumes and camping and Henry. . . . I feel like the Dungeon Master of my life has just told me to Roll for Initiative. I think something big is going to happen.

I run into Henry in the hall before gym, and we plan to meet at my locker at lunch. His turn to pay. When lunch rolls around, I'm practically skipping to get to my locker. But when I get there, the person standing in front of it isn't Henry. It's Bizza.

When she sees me, she gives a hesitant wave. I'm not really mad anymore. There's too much good stuff happening to me to keep all of that anger inside. Plus, I've been so busy with my new friends and sewing and school that I haven't really had time to think about her.

She's wearing a pair of black-and-white striped kneesocks over a pair of red tights and under a pair of cutoff army pants. Her T-shirt has a store-distressed logo of some punk band I remember Barrett talking about in his previous life. Her hair is freshly buzzed, her eyes heavily blackened. When I think about it, she looks pretty goofy.

I don't feel like wasting time waiting for whatever she's come here for, so I say, "Hi. Did you need something?" After

I say it, I realize how cold it sounded, like the only reason she's come to talk to me was to get something from me. I guess that's how it's pretty much been, though, whether it was my brother's table at Denny's or an escort to the STD factory or—

"I just wanted to talk to you for a minute," she says, semi-defensive.

"Don't you have bio now?"

"So? This is important. I need to say it."

I brace myself for some self-absorbed Bizza bullshit, but out comes something unexpected.

"I'm sorry, Jessie. Sorry I used you. Sorry I hurt you. Sorry for being a shitty friend." I move my mouth to say something, but nothing comes out. Bizza continues, "You were my best friend. I mean, you are the best friend I've ever had. Better than I deserved." I can't disagree, so I say nothing. "I don't know if you'll ever forgive me, but I just needed to say it. And thanks for coming with me to the clinic. I don't think I would've gone without you."

"How's *that* situation?" I ask, waving my hand in the general direction of her mouth.

"Better. Gone. And so is Van, too, by the way. I'm not going near that asshole again." She says it like it's not such a big deal, but I can tell that it is from years of her pretending things don't get to Bizza Brickman.

I want to say something snarky about how she shouldn't

have gotten so near that asshole in the first place, but I can't be bothered. Just then Henry walks into the locker section, looking adorable with his curls in his eyes and his giant white shoes. "Hey, Jess," he says, "ready for some grub?"

I look at Bizza to see if she's finished, and she says, "I should get to class, I guess."

Henry smiles at me and says, "I just have to get my jacket. I'll be right back."

After he leaves, Bizza shoulders her backpack and says, "Who's that?"

"A friend," I say. "Definitely a *non*-asshole." She smiles, and I smile back. Part of me is desperate to hug her, like a final, good-bye type of hug, to let her know that I forgive her enough not to hate her anymore.

"Maybe we can hang out sometime," she says.

"Maybe," I say thoughtfully. "I'm pretty busy these days."

She looks slightly hurt, but her Bizza pride is definitely still in tact. "Yeah, me, too, I guess. But maybe when you're not too busy." I nod, and Henry returns. He sticks out a friendly hand to Bizza and says, "Hi, I'm Henry."

Bizza reluctantly shakes it. I watch the two of them. It's as if Bizza shaking hands with Henry is the official transference of my old life to my new one.

"S'later," she says to me, and walks quickly away.

"Ready, m'lady?" Henry bows to me, hand outstretched.

"Yes, m'man," I say, taking his hand.

As we walk, holding hands, he asks, "M'man?"

"You know—m'lady, m'man. Would you have preferred something else?"

"Actually, it was a lot more than I hoped for," and I can see his cheeks turn red underneath his unruly locks of hair.

chapter 35

"DON'T LOOK ANY ROYALTY IN THE
eye. You can only speak when spoken to, unless it's someone
of your station."

"Henry, how am I supposed to know who's royalty and
who's 'of my station'?" I use finger quotes because I can't get
myself to say it like it's part of a normal conversation.

"We'll know. You just walk behind Dottie, and she'll tell
you what to do. And believe me, she'll revel in that."

"Great," I say, although I'm not really worried about that
part. I'd rather someone tell me what to do at this thing than
get put in the stocks for doing something wrong. "Is everyone
going to be really into their characters? Like saying *yay* and
nay and *thou art* and stuff?"

"Some of them will. Usually it's the guys with ponytails.
Don't worry. You're not being graded on this."

If only that were my problem. Henry sees the constipated
look on my face. "What? Did you eat a green french fry? I
hate that."

"No. It's just—" I decide to be honest with him. "Do you
ever feel like a dork doing this? Walking around in a costume

with other people walking around in costumes, holding fake swords, interacting with guys and ponytails and—"

"Jessie, chill," Henry interrupts me. "It's perfectly normal to feel like a dork at Fudwhalla because there's nothing perfectly normal about it. Normally, your average tabletop role-playing geek wouldn't set foot in a live role-playing adventure, but last year Philip told us his cousin was doing it, and we thought it sounded hilarious. It's not often nerds get to make fun of nerds even lower on the nerd food chain."

I clear my throat and look surprised. "You're not a nerd, Henry."

"Nice of you to say, Jess, but I'm not deaf. I've heard people talking crap about me since we morphed into social groups in elementary school. It only sucks when there's no one else around to soften the blow. Of course it bothers me sometimes that I'm not cool. Why do you think I bought new pants?"

We both blush, but probably for different reasons. I feel guilty, like I bullied him into it. "You kind of needed them," I say.

"True, but the only reason I actually went out and bought them was to reduce the nerd factor in your eyes. It worked, I hope?"

"It worked." I smile. "Not that I thought you were a nerd, of course, but you do look better when your pants fit." A *lot* better.

We spend the rest of the meal going over more Fudwhalla

details. I am happy to hear that my new friends thought the whole thing was weird, too. Even though Henry just full-on pronounced his nerd status, the fact that he could and was completely confident about it made me like him even more. I totally respect him. I wonder if I'll ever get to that point myself.

chapter 36

I WAKE EARLY ON THE MORNING OF Fudwhalla. Dottie suggested I eat a big breakfast, since it's always unknown when the first meal will actually get served (and how edible it may be). I'm too nervous for a big breakfast, so I opt for a piece of toast and some scrambled eggs. Dottie came over last night to pick up her skirt. Both of us were impressed at how perfectly the skirts looked and fit. I hope the guys won't be disappointed with their tunics, which we all decided would be fine to hand out when we met up in the morning. Dottie showed me how to wear the corset over my peasant blouse. I felt awkward because you can't really wear a bra under a corset, and therefore, Dottie and I were in my room together topless for the shortest moment while we changed. Not that I looked. The peasant blouse that Dottie lent me is off-white and gathered at the sleeves and around the plunging neckline. It is, as they say, dangerously low-cut, so with the addition of the corset, my cleavage is nicely peeking over the top of the blouse. I felt rather scandalous when I saw myself for the first time, but Dottie swore that's how all the Fudwhalla ladies dress. "I'm telling ya," she said as she changed back into her street clothes, "some bitches get implants just to look hot at Fudwhalla."

"So there will be other females there?" I asked. I had this fear that Dottie and I would be the only girls, and groups of sword-wielding freaks would chase us through a dark forest at night, capture us, and drag us back to their lairs by our hair.

"Oh yeah. I mean, there's the queen, of course, and there's the witches, other royals, their dedicated servants . . ." She darkly smiled at me.

Making breakfast this morning, I feel a little silly with my boobs hanging out, and I pray that no one in my family feels like waking up early to see me off.

I double-check my stuff: sleeping bag, pillow, change of clothes for the ride back. I wanted to bring a flashlight, but Dottie told me there would be torches and lanterns for us to use. More authentic, I guess.

My boobs are dangerously close to a full-on pop-out as I close up my bag, and I barely manage to adjust when I hear Doug's car pull into the driveway. I quickly open the front door so he doesn't have to honk, waking my family into a random boob sighting, which would possibly make them question the innocence of the weekend.

Dottie meets me at the door, and we laughingly acknowledge our ample, jiggling chests. Everyone is already in the car, a minivan that Doug borrowed from his mom. Dottie grabs the tunics, and I lug my bag to the back of the van. Doug pops open the trunk, and I throw my bag inside.

Henry slides open the van's side door from the inside, and when he crouches to avoid hitting his head on the ceiling his eyes are directly in line with my chest. "Um," he stammers, "welcome, m'lady." He quickly averts his gaze, and I manage to slide into the first row of seats. Dottie passes back the tunics, and I hear "Wow" and "Awesome" and "Am I really this fat?"

Kent puts his hand on my shoulder from the backseat and says, "Jessie, thanks for making these. They look fantastic. Really." I beam at a job well done, and then we're off into the wild nerd yonder.

Henry, Doug, and Kent fight over radio stations the whole ride, while Eddie and Philip play various car games, like Slugbug and I Spy. Dottie helps me with my hair. Hers is in several braids, which she has somehow twisted together into an elaborately regal hairstyle. "Yours should be more plain," she tells me, "seeing as you are just the help. Do you know how to French braid?" she asks.

I do. French braiding other people's hair was one of my favorite things to do during fifth-grade recess. Dottie instructed me to part my hair down the middle and give myself two French braids down the back, sort of Ren Fair-y without the flowers. I work on it and notice Henry watching me, although he could just be staring at my boobs. Either way, I'm happy.

When we finally arrive at Fudwhalla, I'm immediately shocked by two things. Number one: There are a lot of people in weird

228

costumes here. And number two: We're in the middle of nowhere. We pulled off the highway, made a bunch of random turns, and ended up at the edge of a huge field with a few buildings scattered around. It's as though we've pulled into the town from *Children of the Corn*, except with more trees, less corn, and, well, no children. I grab my bag in a daze and follow the others between what appear to be two of the four buildings in this "town." Each building is well-labeled with a painted wooden sign: THE INN, THE CASTLE (which pretty much looks the same as The Inn), TOWN HALL, and PRIVIES. I relax a little when I see the last sign, as it means I won't have to poop in the woods after all (if I have to poop, I mean).

People of all shapes and sizes in elaborate costumes of chain mail and velvet mill about. I see several men in tunics, and note how much more original the ones I made look. We head to the town hall to register. Henry walks up beside me, and the first thing I notice (since I didn't really get a good look in the car) is the absence of white shoes (maybe it's the lack of the frightening glow that usually emanates from his feet). Instead, he has some sort of black Doc-esque shoes (thank god he's not wearing some fringy suede boots) tucked under the legs of his black pants. Unlike the many ponytailers (Philip included), Henry's curls hang dashingly around his face. His white shirt, even with the puffy-sleeve factor, is thin enough that it shows off his lean, defined arms. The tunic fits him perfectly, and he really does look kind of dashing. Quite manly, actually, but not in a hairy-chest, mustachey way. Just in a really *good* way.

Registration entails signing in, noting how many guests will be staying in our "house," and receiving a stack of golden coins, which Dottie takes from me and places inside a felt pouch. She then hands the pouch to me and instructs me to tie the bag to the waist of my skirt. I peek inside and notice that the coins all have the word FUDWHALLA printed on them. "Fudwhalla has its own currency?"

"Yeah," Kent answers. "Nigel mints them in his house all year. I can't decide if it's overkill or really cool." I'm voting for overkill, but it is kind of fun. Like traveling to another country inhabited by guys in tights and ponytails.

We walk and we walk, past rainbow-colored tents of other Fudwhalla-goers and various stalls of random medieval ware, until we come to where we'll be parking ourselves for the night. It's a field filled with what appear to be wooden skeletons of one-room houses. Each house is completely bare, only defined by sporadically placed boards around the outside and a sparse formation of boards on top that give the illusion of a roof. They look like someone started a project and neglected to finish it. Maybe the Children of the Corn got to them first. Throughout the field are Fudwhalla-ites, throwing tarps, sheets, and fabrics over the house skeletons. I get an ug feeling in my gut that this may be closer to camping than I thought. "Where are we going, Dottie?" I call to her, since she is now about twenty feet ahead of me and dragging her long skirt farther and farther into the field.

"That's Baroness Radcliffe," she calls back to remind me. "And we're heading toward our home." Noooo.

We pass more tents and more skeleton houses and more sheets and bizarre, medieval-type costumes and strange goatees until we end up on the very edge of the very large field. The skeleton house that Dottie tosses her bag into is butted up against the beginnings of a forest. I turn around to gauge the distance from our house to the very beginning of the field. With the zigzagging through tents and houses, it's at least a good five-minute walk. Plus another five minutes to my most cherished destination—the privies.

"I thought you said we'd be near a bathroom," I kind of whine.

"We are." Eddie laughs, and showcases the entirety of our friendly neighborhood forest.

"For you, maybe, but I don't have the point-and-shoot capabilities of a penis."

"Don't worry about it," the Baroness reassures me. "I'll teach you how to pee in the woods in a really long skirt."

I don't feel the least bit reassured, but things get worse: Our house doesn't have a floor. "Wait—I thought you said we weren't just camping on the ground." I'm really whining now.

"Well, we're sleeping on the ground, but at least we have the house around us," Philip says, pulling flowery bedsheets out of his bag. The guys get to work, covering the ceiling with the sheets to give the appearance of a ceiling and walls. If a

231

roof and walls happened to be covered in hideous orange flowers and did little to protect us from the elements (i.e., frightening forest creatures and knife-wielding children). I sit down inside the house as the sheets go up around me. The sunlight shines through the floral fabric on one of the sides and reminds me of laundry hanging out to dry. Not that I've ever been around laundry hanging outside, because that's a pretty impractical concept in the Midwest, but I imagine this is what it would be like. More pleasant than expected. I lie back and look through our nonexistent roof at the cloud wisps. All of a sudden Henry pops into my sight, ethereal with the sun shining through his curls. He's on a ladder, tossing sheets over the top to create the roof. He waves at me, and I grin back before the flowers float over my view.

I wish I could explain what happened the rest of the day, but I'm a bit confused myself. It seemed like there was some sort of plotline, like the queen was not really a queen and one of the other royals in town was actually the rightful heir. Or something like that. There were all of these messenger types in tights and puffy pants who delivered rolled-up papers from the castle. If we were just sitting around playing D&D, I guess these would have come from the Dungeon Master, but they're essentially the same thing. Based on the messages, we know what's going on in town, who we're supposed to hate, and what it is we should do about it. It was still confusing to me, so mostly I just walked behind the baroness and tended to her needs every time she snapped her fingers. The guys got into their roles, acting like they liked certain people and hated others. I pretend that I am living inside a PBS miniseries (it seems more cultural somehow), but one that isn't in English. I get the gist of things, but mainly I do a lot of following and nodding.

I manage to get in some quality privy time while we're in town, although *quality* is hardly a word I should use around these privies. They are essentially a line of holes in the ground covered by a line of holes to sit on (does anyone really *sit* on those wooden openings?) divided by a line of weak, wooden walls. But at least I have no trouble with my aim.

Day turns to night, and I'm exhausted from being out in the sun all day and following someone's snapping orders. The day ends with a "feast" at the Inn of mainly bread and soup and some corn on the cob (although that ran out quickly and they tried to substitute it with carrots). It is a definite half-assed hodgepodge, but I figure the less I eat, the smaller the chance of a poop in the woods.

By the time our feast is over (should my stomach be growling after a feast?), it's pitch black out except for the town's torches. Thankfully Philip remembered to bring our lantern, but we still barely manage to find our house. It takes many stumbles and one close call of me tripping into the fabric of a house and nearly ripping the wall down before we find our place by the edge of the forest. It is way creepier at night. Now I know how the Hogwarts gang feels when they have to enter the Forbidden Forest. Too bad I left my wand at home.

We line our sleeping bags up inside the house and just manage to fit all seven of us. It's a little too close for comfort, but also slightly comforting to be this close. Who knows what kind of monsters lurk between the trees? (I really should stop with the Stephen King audiobooks.) My sleeping place is next to the "door" on one side and Dottie on the other, with her next to Doug and the rest of the guys down the line. My position is bad for two reasons: One is the fact that there's no one between me and the door if something wicked this way comes, and two is that a slight breeze keeps blowing through the door directly onto my sleeping bag, which of course makes me cold, and which eventually, I'm sure, will make me have to pee.

We sleep in our clothes (which Dottie claims is historically accurate, but I'm just grateful that I don't have to worry about changing in front of these guys). Dottie and I take off our corsets, though, because her mom would kill her if the wire boning got bent in our sleep. Plus, I like to be able to breathe while sleeping. Maybe that's just me, though.

Normally I read or listen to a book in order to fall asleep, but it's so dark in here (and I'm afraid that I'll be attacked if I bring out my—gasp!—iPod). I try to think relaxing thoughts, but it's hard to relax in such a strange place next to such a spooky forest in a tiny fabric house with a group of mainly guys that I've only been friends with for a couple of weeks. It doesn't help that our house is way too quickly filled with the sounds of even breathing (and a little snoring) that lets me know that everyone else is having a perfectly easy time falling asleep.

I wriggle my sleeping bag, and it makes that slithery, crispy sleeping bag sound. The wind blows. I wriggle. Blows. Wriggle. Repeat. And I realize I really have to pee. What am I supposed to do? I don't have a flashlight, and the lantern is out. Dottie taught me earlier how to pee from a tree: Hug the tree with both arms, plant your feet around the base of the tree, and lean back. Guaranteed not to pee on your feet, she says. But how am I even supposed to find a tree? It's so dark. Dark and scary and crackly and—

I sit up. My sleeping bag makes a quick, slick noise. I can't sit here all night without peeing, but I'm petrified of going out into the dark alone. What other choice do I have? Wetting my sleeping bag (and the clothes I have to wear again tomorrow) doesn't sound like the best plan. I'm going to have to brave the forest.

I quietly unzip my sleeping bag and try to make as little noise as possible when I stand up. It's so dark that I have to feel around for the door, and even when my hand finds fabric I'm not sure if it will get me out of here or bring the whole building down. I accidentally knock my knuckle on one of the wooden beams and automatically blurt, "Shit!"

"Jessie?" a whisper comes from the other end of the house (i.e., less than ten feet away).

"Yeah? Who's that?" I whisper back.

"Henry. What are you doing?"

"I have to pee." I sort of hope that our whisper conversation rouses Dottie so she can go with me. No luck, as I hear her snort, roll over, and snort again.

235

"Do you need a light?" Henry asks.

"Yes, please. It's so dark." I hear him rustle around on the ground, then a wrapper crinkles, a pop, and a green glow hovers in Henry's hand. "A glow stick? Did they have those in medieval times?" I joke.

"Let's just say it's a magic wand," he whispers.

He gestures like he's going to toss it, but I stop him with, "No! I don't want it to hit anyone. I can't see where my hands are to catch it."

"Hold on," he says, and I follow the stick as it unzips Henry's sleeping bag. I can see the faint glow of his bare chest.

He tucks himself under the fabric flap nearest him, and I hear twigs crack as he makes his way along the outside of our house. I manage to find my way out of the door without pain this time, and I meet him in the green light.

"Will you come with me?" I ask desperately.

"To pee?" He sounds embarrassed.

"You don't have to watch—or listen, thank you—but I don't want to go into the forest alone. Please?" I'm making a pathetic, pleading face, but I doubt he can see it.

"All right. But can you do it fast? It's cold."

He finds my hand in the dark and leads us into the forest with his glow stick guiding the way. I want to be several trees deep in case someone sees. I spot a perfectly sized tree for the grab-and-lean. "Now go stand over there," I tell him. He

236

starts to walk away, but the darkness envelops me. "Wait! Come back. You have to stand closer. But you can't look or listen."

"Jessie, believe me, I don't want to watch you pee, but how am I supposed to not hear it?"

"Cover your ears and hum something."

"Hum what?" he asks, and I'm desperate to start peeing.

"'I'm a Little Teapot!' Go! Start humming!" Henry turns away, covers his ears and hums. I hike up my skirt, wrap myself around the tree, and go. I hum along with Henry in hopes that it helps cover up the pit-pat sound my pee makes on the forest floor.

When I am absolutely finished, I yell-whisper, "Okay!" but Henry is too in the humming groove to notice. I walk up to him, yank the glow stick out of his hand, and tap him on the head with it. "Poof. You can stop humming now."

"All done?" he asks.

"No, I'm still going, but I thought I'd let you stop humming. Careful, I might get it on your shoes."

He smiles a giant, sweet smile, and I know now that I *want* all of those dreams I've been having to come true. At first, the old me doesn't quite know how to handle the situation, but Imalthia reminds me that I'm not such a wuss after all. I boldly lean in and kiss him. At first Henry tentatively kisses me back, then brings his hands up and cradles my face. We kiss each other in the green glow of the Forbidden Forest.

"Mmmm," I say as we float apart. "That girl from band camp was right."

"Hmmm?" he asks, but he kisses me again before I need to answer. If this is what kissing a nerd is like, I don't know why I ever bothered trying to be cool.

When we are sufficiently kissed out and weak-kneed from standing, I say, "We should probably get some sleep. Who knows what weird stuff we're going to have to do tomorrow." He feels for my hand to hold, but I say, "Uh, better not. I think I may have peed on my hand a little earlier."

"I'm so glad you told me this *now*."

"I didn't touch you with it!"

"I know. I mean, I'm glad you told me now instead of before we kissed. 'I peed on my hand' doesn't really set the mood, you know?"

"For some people it might," I blather as we make our way back to the house.

"Jessie," Henry says as we get to the door, "good night," and he leans in for one more soft kiss.

He holds the door open for me, and I raise the glow stick high in the air as he climbs over bodies and into his sleeping bag. I tuck into mine, clutching the glow stick to my chest until it fades out and I fall asleep.

When I wake up to the welcome light of morning, I don't remember any of my dreams. But who needs dreams?

chapter 37

SUNDAY IS A WHIR OF WEIRD-
ness, and I find myself involved in a chase after Dottie the
Baroness "accidentally" pours porridge onto the queen's head.
(I have no idea if this was written on one of our messages,
only that Dottie yelled, "Run!" and I am always supposed to
do what she says.) We run through the town, past the stalls
and tents, then into the field, darting between houses. It's a
little terrifying being chased, even if it is fake, but it's also a
total rush. I'm laughing and screaming the entire way.

We eventually end up in the forest, ducking behind a tree.
Just as we hear the drum of footsteps approaching, a bell clangs
in the distance. Dottie instantly pops out of hiding and yells
(to our pursuers, I assume), "Too slow, bitches! Game over!" I
hesitantly stand, but Dottie is already heading out of the forest. I follow her, my skirt hiked up in my hands.

"What's going on?" I yell after her. "Is it over?"

She turns around and says, "High noon. You can turn
back into a pumpkin now."

"Did we win?" I ask, totally confused.

"No one got hurt, and no one got captured, so I guess so."

I don't know if I'll ever get this, but that's okay. Maybe I don't need to get an A in everything.

Back at the house, I'm about to pull the fabric down off the frame when Doug yells, "Wait! We need somewhere to change." I forgot that we brought regular clothes to change into for the ride home. As uncomfortable and slutty as my costume is, I'm going to miss wearing it. Maybe it's *because* it's uncomfortable and slutty.

Dottie and I head into the house first and change. "Shit," Dottie sighs, "I forgot a bra." Thankfully I remembered mine, and I put it on along with a pair of jeans, a T-shirt, and a hoodie. I slip my knee-high boots back on and tuck them under my jeans. It's the guys' turn to change, and I meet Henry on his way in. He still looks adorable, his hair a little crazy from the lack of washing, and his pants and shoes dusty. He looks at me in my regular clothes. "You're back," he says, and I detect a note of disappointment.

"You wanted me to wear that costume forever?"

He shrugs. "Can you blame me? You looked pretty hot."

"Thanks. So how do I look now?" I ask sarcastically.

"Equally hot," he recovers, "just less exposed." Henry gently flicks one of my French braids, which I decided to keep in for the rest of the day. "I like your hair like this," he muses. "It frames your face beautifully." I blush and wish the two of us were still alone in the green light of the glow stick. Kent lets out a huge burp, and I know we're not.

I kick Henry's black shoe with my boot. "Maybe you can wear these sometimes, you know, instead of your white gym shoes?" I don't mean to, but I scrunch my nose at the mention of his white gym shoes.

"You don't like my white gym shoes?"

"To be honest, not really. They're just so—white."

Henry laughs. "That they are. I never really thought about it. Maybe you can go shopping with me for some new shoes."

"Only if you want to, of course." I don't want him to think I'm trying to completely change him. At the same time, I can't help what I'm attracted to. No one can, right?

"I need some new shoes anyway. I grew out of the white ones last month."

"Shoe shopping. It's a date." I take his hands and swing them gently while we talk.

"And maybe while we're out, we can find you another corset."

"In your dreams," I say, although, technically, it's in mine.

We finish packing up as we sip on warm Coke that we left in the van. Everyone is a little quiet from exhaustion and the realization that the weekend is finally over. Before we get into the van, Kent announces, "I'd just like to say that this year's Fudwhalla would not have been what it was were it not for the glorious sewing skills of Jessie Sloan. I raise this warm Coke to you, Jessie. Huzzah!" Everyone else raises their Cokes, too. "Huzzah!" They repeat. "Huzzah!"

chapter 38

IT'S HOMECOMING WEEKEND, AND
my friends and I have decided that instead of some of us going
to the dance and others staying home, we'd make it a Dungeons
and Dragons marathon weekend. Henry's parents are home
Saturday night, so we decide to play at my house. My parents
promise to leave just as soon as Barrett and Chloe pose for one
more round of photos (the previous rounds being in the living
room, the backyard, and the garden, with the current round
taking place in front of Barrett's car because Dad says, "When
you look back at these pictures in twenty years, you'll laugh at
how classic your car was!"). Barrett looks great in a powder
blue tux, complete with ruffley shirt and polished white shoes
(which are acceptable due to the kitsch factor), and Chloe looks
gorgeous in a vintage mauve dress with a full pleated skirt that
hits just below her knees. Throughout the painfully long photo
session, my friends are dropped off at our house. First Kent,
then Philip, then Doug and Dottie, and lastly Henry's mom
drops off Henry and Eddie. My parents pause from the photo
extravaganza to wave at their parents, and my friends gather in
a clump on the lawn to watch the homecoming couple.

"We really have to go," Barrett tells Mom and Dad. "We're picking up two other couples. That means more pictures at their houses. It would be nice to actually get to the dance, seeing as we bothered dressing up and all."

"Okay, okay," Dad submits. "Pretend you're helping Chloe into the car. Then pretend you're getting in the car."

"Whatever you say, Dad. And after that we're going to pretend to drive away."

Henry, looking supercute in his new black Chucks, holds my hand as we watch the beautiful couple. Everyone waves at Barrett and Chloe as they pull out of the driveway, giving them a proper homecoming send-off.

"Hey!" my dad yells excitedly. "Why don't you guys get together for some shots?"

"Sure," Dottie says in her droll voice. "Why not?"

The seven of us huddle together, arms wrapped around one another's shoulders and backs.

"Smile!" Dad yells. Henry tugs on one of my braids, while my dad snaps away. When he's finished, Philip says, "Mr. Sloan—think you can e-mail those to me? I want to post them on my blog."

"Sure thing," Dad says.

My parents go out to a movie, while Dottie leads us in a fully intense adventure. After decimating some pizzas, we've had to solve a riddle, disarm a trap, and discover the whereabouts of an ancient sword. There has been a lot of talking and thinking, but not a whole lot of action. We're in the depths of an endless tunnel, and there's anticipation in the air. Imalthia feels along the tunnel wall until she discovers a secret handle. She turns it and walks into a room she didn't know existed before.

There's a lengthy pause, punctuated by Kent gnawing on a pizza crust. Then Dottie smirks. "Roll for initiative," she commands.

Something big is going to happen.

Acknowledgments

Huge, gigantic thanks to the following people:

Liz, for being an amazing editor and friend.

Rich, for the fantabulous cover art and hilarious e-mails.

Nina, for the neverending supply of all things Dungeons and Dragons.

My students, Meredith, Eleanor, Michael, Daniel, Matt, and Hannah, for reading my books and always coming back.

Eastman, for the advice and countless e-mails.

My old friends, Beth, Liz, Ali, and Tracy, for filling my teen years with stuff, good and bad, that I can twist into books.

Wendy, for the inspiration.

Mom, for the love.

Amy, for being the best sis.

Romy, for coming along when you did.

Matt, for all of the above and everything else.

GOFISH

JULIE HALPERN

There are all kinds of nerds to choose from, so why Dungeons and Dragons? Have you played D&D? If so, you've got to tell us about your character.

I played D&D for the first time in high school, with two metal-head friends on a blustery winter evening. It was so fun! But then I didn't play again until college, which is the perfect place to play—in a dorm, where you don't even have to go outside to find other people, with no curfew and unlimited pizza delivery.

My characters have varied. When I originally started playing, I wanted to be a fancy, charismatic, magic-using elf. But that involved too much thinking. So then my second character was a large-boned fighter named "Sofa." These days, I run the Dungeons and Dragons Club at the school where I work, which is insanely fun. My character is an elf bard named "Lulabelle" who makes oven mitts and plays the recorder at inappropriate times. I do quite a bit of DMing (dungeon mastering) in the club as well. I'm pretty good at it. Especially doing different voices for the NPCs (non-player characters).

Jessie seems to have a pervasive fear of needing to poo at inconvenient times. Not to be too graphic, but is this a personal fear?

Funny that stood out to you. And, yes, that was sort of a fear in my past. In the *Get Well Soon* days of my life (when I was deeply depressed), I had this fear of needing to go and not having a place to do it. And the camping piece is all true—I did go to a live-action role-playing thing (LARP) and worry about having to poo in the woods. But I actually did have a poo-in-the-woods experience when I was a librarian at a private school in Chicago, and I went on a camping trip with my seventh graders. Imagine having to wake up in the middle of the night to go to the bathroom in the woods, wondering if a thirteen-year-old is going to pop his head out of a tent at any minute. These days, I just try not to put myself in situations where there's no bathroom nearby.

How was the LARP? Did you only go once?

I was in Denmark. I was with my Danish friend Louise. Everyone there was Danish. I do not speak Danish. I actually just played Louise's chambermaid, or whatever, and trailed along after her. And I was so freaked out by the idea of having to sleep in a "house" with a group of huge Danish dudes that I didn't even know, that Louise and I spent the first night on the floor of one of the actual buildings near the campsites. After that, I took a train back to her apartment, and she stayed for two more days and LARPed it up. I think I interrupted her roommate's romantic weekend with her out-of-town boyfriend, too. It was not the best LARPing experience. Did I mention the black slugs in the camping field that were as big as mice?

Your descriptions of Jessie's handmade skirts were excellent! Do you make your own clothes?

The only time I really made my clothes was when I lived in Australia. I lived right near this road where there were tons of fabric shops, all extremely cheap. Since all I had with me when I went to Australia was a giant backpack filled with practical backpacker clothes, when I actually settled down in one spot in Melbourne for a while, I wanted some more interesting clothes to wear. That's when I started to make my skirts. They were hand-sewn—practically disposable they were done so poorly—but the fabrics were brilliant. I had this one that was covered in frightening clown heads. And I bought some fabric for Luna Park, an amusement park that was closed down in Sydney at the time but still open and a little seedy in Melbourne. I thought it was fantastic that they actually had fabric for the place! I still haven't made anything with it, and I've had it for thirteen years. It'll have to be something pretty great to use it. Maybe I can make my daughter's wedding gown out of it. Would that be weird?

What's your favorite outfit/thing to wear?
Gym shoes. I LOVE colorful gym shoes, preferably Converse or Vans. The vice principal of my school called me the Imelda Marcos of tennis shoes just yesterday. I also love hoodies. Lately I've been into buying expensive brands of jeans, which is a new thing. So—jeans, gym shoes, and hoodies. I'm not very fancy.

What's the nerdiest thing you've ever done?
The truth is that I don't really consider myself a nerd. I just like a lot of different things, and some of them are considered nerdy by others. What would other people consider the nerdiest thing I've done? Maybe that live role-playing thing. Or maybe that I went to the San Diego Comic-Con as part of my honeymoon? We also went to the restaurant where Large Marge sent Pee Wee in *Pee Wee's Big Adventure*. Nothing nerdy about that. I don't think.

If you could travel in time, where would you go?
I would go to the 1893 World's Columbian Exposition! I just love the idea of being that excited by things before they were

commonplace. Electricity! Art! People from around the globe! And it's my city, Chicago, at its most welcoming. Although I don't know what I'd wear.

What was your first job?
Babysitter. Then I was a checker at a discount drug mart called F&M, which I referred to as "F&Poo." Clever, I know.

Which do you like better: cats or dogs?
I like my cat to the extreme, but I guess I like the idea of dogs more. I am definitely not a person who goes up to animals and oohs and aaahs and pets them. I'm a little scared of animals if I don't know them. Because animals can't talk and tell me what I'm doing to them that they don't like. But they can bite me.

What do you value most in your friends?
Loyalty, sincerity, and humor. I have friends that I have had since I was three years old, and I make new friends pretty easily, too. I like to laugh, but not at others' expenses. Well, maybe occasionally at someone else's expense.

What's your favorite song?
"I Am a Scientist" by Guided by Voices

Who is your favorite fictional character?
Buffy the Vampire Slayer

You're a fan of *Buffy the Vampire Slayer*. So: Angel or Spike?
Wonderful timing for this question, since I have recently started watching *Buffy* again for the eight millionth time. I even went out and spent $60 on *Buffy* comics. Who said I wasn't a nerd? Anyway, I am almost 100% Team Spike. I like the size of Angel and the way he and Buffy interact, but otherwise he is kind of a dud.

Spike is so funny and passionate and devoted—and pathetic—but still, as a fictional character, unquestionably appealing.

Can you play any instruments? Have you ever been in a band: garage or otherwise?
I can play the piano, and in various capacities, the bass guitar and cello. I would definitely need a refresher on how to read music, but after that I could probably pick up things relatively easily. I don't think I could ever be a good improviser with an instrument though.

Are you a morning person or a night owl?
Morning person completely. I have pretty bad sleep issues that prevent staying up even remotely late at night. Most days I wake up ready to go.

What's your idea of the best meal ever?
Lou Malnati's deep-dish pizza; my grandma's broccoli-spinach casserole; cream soda; chicken soup with rice; French silk pie; a piece of yellow cake frosted with buttercream; various cookies of the sprinkled, smiley-faced, chocolate-chip, oatmeal-scotchie variety; and some sort of ice-cream treat. I just had breakfast, so I'm too full to think of more. Or is this enough?

Lillian and her BFF, Josh, are on a cross-country road trip to find their friend Penny, who may or may not have faked her own kidnapping. But Lil's more interested in finding out whether or not Josh loves her —because she's in love with him.

DON'T STOP NOW

FRIEND OR BOYFRIEND?

JULIE HALPERN

AUTHOR OF GET WELL SOON

Find out if Lil and Josh are meant to be in

DON'T STOP NOW

by **JULIE HALPERN**

CHAPTER ONE

I did it," Penny's voice whispers on my voicemail. Confused, I push the button to replay.

"I did it." That's all she said. According to Robot Phone Woman Time Keeper, Penny called at exactly 4:47 a.m., a rather unacceptable time to call anyone on a Saturday morning, and most certainly not on the Saturday morning after the Friday that was our last day of high school EVER. Because it is the first Saturday of the rest of our lives, finally past all of the clique clack crud of high school, I allow myself to sleep past my mother's acceptable sleep hour of exactly 11:59 ("At least it's still morning") until 1:43 in the afternoon. Which makes me approximately nine hours too late to stop Penny.

How did it become my responsibility to help this pathetic soul anyway? We weren't ever friends until this past year, and even then only by default. I had no choice really, unless I wanted to be a total hag by not asking her to join us at the Lunch Table of Misfit Toys, dubbed so by our paltry group of seniors in lunch period 8 who were so placed because we chose not to stress ourselves out with AP classes, resulting in a more pliable schedule for the admin to have their way with. Instead of the race for the maximum number of AP credits possible, I selected some easy, breezy independent studies of things I actually enjoy doing, like Creative Writing and Photo. Why bother with the AP BS anyway? So you can graduate college early? No thanks. I breezed through my senior year like I plan to breeze through this summer, living off the fat of the land that is my bat mitzvah savings, and just chilling out. No worries. Or at least, that was the plan.

"I did it." Who leaves a message like that? Who is so paranoid that they have to be so cryptic? If this wasn't day one of my Summer of Nothing, I might be in a hurry to figure this out. But first: breakfast. Or lunch, really. Snack? Lack, or lunk maybe. It is a bowl of cereal, whatever it is. I like to fancy myself a cereal connoisseur. Today, slightly out of it and in need of substance *and* energy, I mix some Frosted Mini-Wheats with Cookie Crisp, and throw in a few Craisins for fruit and texture. I shake up the skim milk, splash it on, toss around the cereal pieces with a spoon to make sure each piece is coated with milk, and plant myself in front of the computer. Then I second-guess it. Maybe I don't want my lunk interrupted by the possibility of more Penny drivel waiting on the other side of the screen, so I flip on the TV instead. An actual video is on MTV. Hip-hop or rap or something. Not my scene. But I can't help wishing I had a butt like that girl in the video. I wonder how she buys jeans, though.

"I did it." It's like Penny's voice is floating out of my cereal from between the flakes and the crisps. How did she say it? It wasn't urgent or terrified, like someone calling 911 from under her bed as she waits for a killer to enter her room, nor was it excited or light or distracted or a million other adjectives I can think of. She just sounded flat, like the only reason she left the message at all was to keep a record of her existence.

Before I call Penny, you know, just to clarify things, I decide to call my best friend, Josh. Although, if there's one person who can outsleep me, it's him, and I say this from experience. Sadly the experience is due to the fact that he and I are so platonic that his dad and my mom could give a rat turd if I sleep at his house or he sleeps at mine. On the couch, of course. So damn pathetic, then, that I am so madly in love with him. Cliché, touché, but true. I've spent four years waiting for something to happen between us that is more than just sharing a toothbrush when he forgets to bring his own. This summer is the last chance, before I head off to college and he heads off to tour Europe with his band or records the Next Big Thing album he always talks about or possibly moves to Saskatoon to hunt moose. He doesn't know where he'll go, but it sure isn't college.

And it's most definitely not in any way, shape, or form dependent on anything I do or anywhere I go. But, damn, I wish it was.

I decide to try and wake him. The phone only rings twice before Josh picks up.

"Heeeyyyy." He sounds awake and happy to see me on the caller ID, which gives my stomach a buzz. I remember once at school when I was talking to some randomer, and Josh comes out of the bathroom, me not expecting to see him there because he had Español at the time, and this randomer, upon seeing the two of us see each other, says, "It's like you guys haven't seen each other in weeks. That's how happy you look." And I thought, *Him, too?*

"Good afternoon, sir. May I interest you in a pointless quest?" Josh and I like to go for long walks or drives with fake purposes and dub them quests. Once we spent an entire afternoon "looking for love in all the wrong places," like that super-lame old country song. We'd look under rocks, at Ben & Jerry's, in the sand box at Stroger Park. I thought maybe, just maybe, he'd get the hint that love was standing right next to him in a cute pair of cut-offs, but Josh seemed to miss that somehow.

"I'll meet you at Stroger in twenty. And I hope you don't mind, but I have evening stink." Josh isn't much of a fan of showering on a regular basis, which may put off some, but I prefer his sleep smell to some covered-up soap smell any day.

I finish my cereal, drop the bowl in the sink, and tug on a blue bra, blue T-shirt, and jean shorts. Some days I like to be monochromed, just for the hell of it. I brush my teeth, tug my chin-length golden brown hair into a nub of a ponytail, shuffle my way into a pair of flip-flops, and I'm out the door.

The air smells free. Free from class schedules and guidance counselors and hallway politics. High school hell is over.

"I did it." Damn that message. Damn Penny for glomming her way into my life. I wish I didn't care. It's messing with my new freedom vibe.

Three blocks away is Stroger Park, big when I was little and little now that I'm, well, big. Two regular swings, a tire swing, two baby swings, a slide, a wall climb, some monkey bars, and plenty of woodchips to stick in your flip-flops. I always wondered why the woodchips. It seemed like there would be more woodchip-in-the-eye accidents than woodchips-as-saviors-for-falling-children incidents. Or maybe I just missed them because I was too busy, you know, being a kid.

Josh hangs upside down from the monkey bars, shirtless (as is his summer look), his self-cut, shoulder-length brown hair dangling below him. I try not to ogle, but, damn, he looks amazing without a shirt. How do guys get to look so good without exercising or eating well at all?

He's skinny, but not too skinny, and all nice and defined. I exhale a platonic sigh.

"Hey, Lil," he calls and swings himself off the bars, stumbling onto the woodchips. Even graceless, he's gorgeous. "You smell that?" he asks as I approach him, and I sit down on the metal ladder to the monkey bars.

"Well, what do you expect when you don't shower?" I ask.

"No." He chuckles in his slow, slack way. He grabs the high bar closest to me and hangs himself so he can easily kick my knees with his ratty black Chucks. "Not me." He takes a huge sniff of air. "*That*. That smell. The rest of our lives." He grins big and I grin bigger. Our lives are going somewhere away from here. *Like Penny*, I remember.

"I got a message. This morning. From Penny."

"Poor little lamb." Josh always teases me about Penny because I befriended her out of pity, but he plays along, too. We're both too nice to let her go it alone. "What'd she say?" he asks me, still hanging.

I ignore the shoes on my knees. "'I did it.'" I look up at him and whisper it the same way she whispered to my voicemail.

"Did what?" he asks, but not curious enough. "*It?*" He laughs, although we both know she did *it* a long time ago, thanks to the pregnancy scare aftermath I had to clean up.

"She told me she was going to do something the other night, before graduation. Only I was just half listening, and you know how morose she can be. Sometimes I just need to block her out if I want to have a bit of fun." Josh nods and lets the flappy rubber of his messed-up shoe tug on my knee.

"So what did she do?" He's more interested now, and now that I've got an audience for the story, so am I.

"If I heard her right . . ." I pause, adding to the tension of the tale I'm about to begin. "Well." Quizzical look. Pause. "I think she may have faked her own kidnapping."

CPSIA information can be obtained
at www.ICGtesting.com
Printed in the USA
LVHW040137141218
600368LV00003B/403